To Rhonda

SWAMP ANGEL

"I am crucified with Christ: nevertheless I live; yet not I, but Christ liveth in me: and the life which I now live in the flesh I live by the faith of the Son of God, who loved me, and gave himself for me." Galatians 2:20 KJV

God Bless!
Kay Chandler

Kay Chandler

Multi-Award-Winning Author

Ja 33:3

This is a work of fiction. Characters, places and incidents are the products of the author's imagination or are used fictitiously.

Scripture taken from the King James Version of the Holy Bible

Cover Design by Chase Chandler

DEDICATED TO VERNON LEWIS, SR.

I dedicate this book in memory of a dear man whom I never had the pleasure of meeting. I met his sweet daughter, Verna Hendrix, when she became a reader of my novels and ordered signed books for her daddy. Not only was he a voracious reader, but he instilled that same love for books in his children..

Vernon was an Alabama Plow Man—a hard worker who was happiest digging in the rich South Alabama soil—but at the end of the day, he grabbed a book. I felt honored that he chose mine.

Earl Vernon Lewis, 85, plowed his last row and departed this life September 28, 2021. Rest in peace, dear sir.

SWAMP ANGEL

For those who have read other Kay Chandler novels, you may recognize familiar old friends in this story. However, the book is written as a standalone. So whether this is your introduction to the characters, or if you met Cooper and Carly Flanigan and conniving Pearl Greene in PLOW HAND; or Gracie and Garth Graham in UNWED; or the orphan teen, Ludie, in MERCY—I hope you'll be blessed by following their redemptive story in SWAMP ANGEL.

CHAPTER 1

September 3 1949.
Cartersville, Georgia

It wasn't turning out to be the wedding of her dreams—certainly not the way she had imagined it would be. But there was very little in Ludie Graham's life that had ever turned out the way she imagined.

Her stomach wrenched when her intended drove past a beautiful church, then stopped two blocks over in front of a building with a Neon sign flashing, 'Bottoms Up Bar.' He crawled out of the truck, opened her door and announced, "This is it. There's a room in the back where weddings are performed."

Ludie felt a tinge of apprehension as they strode hand-in-hand through the smoke-filled juke joint with a bar full of drunks, all glaring and hee-hawing.

She stopped short seeing the words, 'Wedding Chapel,'

painted in crude letters above a door to a back room. He tugged at her hand and led her inside, then closed the door behind them. The only furnishings consisted of four folding chairs and a wooden podium. A picture of Jesus knocking on a door hung catty-wompas on the back wall.

Ludie attempted to relax when he put his arm around her and gently squeezed her shoulder. When their gaze locked, her heart melted like hot butter. Never had she seen a more handsome fellow and in a few short minutes he'd belong to her. *Mrs. Schooner Alexander. . . Ludie Alexander.* Regardless of how she said it, it sounded good.

"Happy, darlin'?"

She nodded, though she felt confident if she spoke she would be unable to stop the tears struggling to come out. Garth and Gracie Graham had been good to her. They had taken her into Nine Gables Orphanage in Goat Hill, Alabama, and loved her as their own, eventually adopting her into their family. It was only after she met Schooner that the trouble between them began.

Garth was a great father and had never raised his voice at her, but he was furious when he learned she'd fallen in love. Ludie had always had a short fuse, yet she'd never spoken to either Garth or Gracie the way she did prior to leaving.

But they were wrong to try and stop her. Weren't they? Regardless of where the blame lay, having her wedding take place without them was almost too much to bear.

For several years, she had imagined a lovely wedding in the

church with Garth standing by her side. When the preacher would ask, "Who gives this woman away," Garth would proudly step forward and say, "Her mother and I." The beautiful thought always made her feel warm inside. To think she had someone to give her away meant she finally belonged to someone.

Ludie glanced down at her brightly colored cotton-print dress. It was fine for wearing to town on Saturday afternoon, but it was far from being the gorgeous white dress of her dreams. If only she could look like a real bride and see Schooner's face light up while watching her walk down the aisle of a church.

How many times had she imagined hearing the words, "I now pronounce you man and wife." Her handsome groom would lift her veil and the congregation would cheer and clap. The happy couple would run out of the church to live happily ever after. But the only part of this day that matched up with her dream wedding was the handsome groom. It was hard to believe they'd known each other for such a short time, yet it was long enough to know they were head over heels in love. Shouldn't that be enough?

The first sentence to one of her favorite novels came to mind. Ludie finally understood what it meant to be living in the best of times and the worst of times. In a matter of minutes, she'd become Mrs. Schooner Alexander—wife of the sweetest, most loving man she'd ever known—but at the same time, she had managed to hurt the two people who had loved her unconditionally. She rubbed her hand across her lips. *Unconditionally?* No! She was wrong. Wrong to hurt them, but also wrong to think there was nothing she could do to make them stop loving her. Regrettably, she had succeeded.

The awful, angry names that spewed from her lips just before running out the door and crawling into Schooner's truck would haunt her forever.

Schooner was shy, but if he'd only gone inside to meet them as she pleaded with him to do, instead of waiting in the truck, Garth and Gracie would've understood why she fell in love at first sight with such a sweet guy. They insisted she needed to know more about him, but she knew all she needed to know and would have a whole lifetime for her handsome husband to fill in the blanks.

Her thoughts were interrupted when the door to the back room opened. The young fellow wearing a white shirt and black bow-tie who had been minding the bar in the front, came strutting through the door of the so-called wedding chapel.

Strutting behind him were a couple of shady-looking characters. Ludie looked at Schooner for an explanation. Where was the preacher and shouldn't they inform these three hoodlums that a wedding was about to take place?

She was taken aback when the fellows congratulated Schooner with slaps on the back and hee-hawed as if they'd come to enjoy a comedy show. Schooner said, "Fellows, meet my bride. This is the lovely Ludie Graham. Hon, shake hands with Brute. He's gonna perform our ceremony."

Ludie's jaw dropped, though Schooner didn't seem to notice her stunned reaction.

"The big guy is Ox, and the red-headed dude is called Grander, and once you know them, you'll understand why folks thinks he's grander."

The bartender's wicked grin sent chills down her spine.

"She'll do fine, Schooner. A little on the skinny side, but not bad at all." He stretched out his hand, though she refused to accept it.

She shook her head voraciously. "No, Schooner. I want a preacher to marry us. Not some bartender."

A big galoot of a man that Schooner referred to as Ox attempted to shame her. "I'm appalled at your holier-than-thou attitude, ma'am. Preacher Boy, here, has to moonlight to make ends meet. His congregation is made up of po' folks who can't pay him a decent wage. Surely, you don't fault him for having to hold down two jobs."

Ignoring the comment, her eyes traveled from the top of the so-called preacher's cowboy hat, down to his worn boots. "Are you a preacher who tends a bar, or a bartender who preaches?"

The man licked his lips and grinned. "Your remark seems to wreak of animosity, ma'am, and that troubles me greatly. I sincerely hope you aren't insinuating you have something against preachers. Why, they're almost as good as bartenders. My grandma said whatever God calls good is gotta be good. This ain't my first rodeo, sugar foot. I'm known as Brother Brute in these parts and these other two fine fellows are here to witness this joyous occasion. Now, if ever'body is ready, we need to get this show on the road before I lose my paying job."

What kind of preacher was named Brute? Was this one big ugly joke? Ludie's instinct told her to run to the nearest bus station and catch the first bus going to Goat Hill, Alabama. Gazing into Schooner's eyes, she said, "I'm sorry. I don't think I can go through with—"

He instantly placed his hands on either side of her face and kissed her. Not just a peck on the cheek, but a long and passionate kiss on the lips. Her knees turned to jelly and her heart hammered so fast she could almost hear it beating. He looked dreadfully handsome with his black, curly hair falling in ringlets over his dark brown eyes.

Before she had a chance to finish her sentence, Brute said, "Miss Ludie Graham, do you take this man and promise to love, obey, cherish, and all that other stuff for as long as you both shall live? If so, say you do."

"I do."

"Schooner Alexander, do you take this beautiful woman to be your awfully wedded wife?"

The two witnesses snickered.

Ludie winced. "Excuse me, but I think you meant to say lawfully wedded, not awfully wedded."

Schooner's lip curled, "That's what he said, hon." He shifted on his feet. "I do, Brother Brute. Now, are we done?"

"Not until we all kiss the bride. The groom first, of course."

CHAPTER 2

On the other side of town . . .

September 3rd. Carly Flanigan glared at the date on the calendar until the mounting tears blurred her vision. Hearing the sudden sound of rain battering the tin roof, she lumbered over to the kitchen window to check on little Emma. The drenched child ran around the yard, stomping in every mud puddle. Normally, Carly would've insisted the child come inside, but nothing about September 3rd would ever be normal.

It had been three years since that fateful day. She couldn't count the times she'd been advised by well-meaning friends to get on with her life. Easy for them to say. How does one overcome such a terrible loss, when accompanied by such an overriding sense of guilt? No one understands. Not even Cooper. She'd tried to pray, but the words always got stuck in her throat. "Father, I need your help. I can't do this. Every time I try—"

An eerie, unexplainable chill swept over her. Twirling around, she expected to see someone standing behind her, though there was no one there. Then, shaking her head with a vengeance, she muttered, "No. I won't do it. I can't!" Was her mind playing tricks, or could it be a force stronger than her own urging her to enter the nursery she had purposely avoided for thirty-six agonizing months.

The broom in her hand fell to the floor. Carly stepped over it, with her head telling her to turn back, and her heart bidding her to enter. Or was it the other way around? But why now? What purpose could it possibly serve? Hadn't she suffered enough?

For months, Cooper had encouraged—even pleaded with her to let him strip the closed-off room of the nursery furnishings and repaint it, saying it would help bring closure. But he was wrong. There could never be closure. She wanted to turn away, and she wasn't at all sure why she didn't.

She swallowed hard, as she slowly turned the knob. Then, drawing a deep breath, she stepped into the small area she hadn't entered since—since it happened. After forcing her gaze to absorb every detail in the tiny room, Carly braced her back against the wall, then slowly slid down on the floor and wept.

Some days she could manage to carry on, but on days like today, all she wanted to do was cry. Had she not been so careless, her baby boy would now be three years old. She hadn't had a good night's sleep in three years. How many times had she awakened in a cold sweat in the middle of the night with the same dream, standing before a judge. He'd rap a gavel on the podium and shout a guilty verdict. *Murder!* Did she deserve anything less?

Sitting cross-legged on the floor, the horrible memories swished back and forth in her head like garments being tossed to and fro in a washing machine, leaving her with the feeling of being wrung out to dry. But the longer she sat reminiscing, the more she realized it was impossible to bring up the dreadful past without remembering the good times along the way. Like the day she and Cooper settled on a name for the baby. She reached up and touched her lips. How long had it been since she smiled?

Heartwarming memories—long ago buried—resurfaced with a freshness akin to the lingering smell of sunshine on freshly laundered sheets. Coop had suggested if it were a boy, they'd name him Dugan in memory of Carly's late husband, Julian Dugan. If a girl, she'd be called Julie. Her smile quickly faded. Choking on the tears, she whispered, "I'm sorry, my sweet little Duggie. Mama is so sorry."

At the sound of footsteps on the porch, she winced. Heavenly days! Could it be noon, already? Where had the time gone?

She jerked the tail of her apron up to her face to dry her tears, and rushed to the kitchen, just as Cooper walked in. He hung his cap on a nail and bent over the stove, sniffing the covered pot, the way he always did at lunch. In the past Carly thought it amusing the way he wanted to guess the contents before lifting the lid. She loved the way his face would light up, reminding her of a kid opening a present at Christmas. It was sweet the way he never seemed disappointed, regardless of what she'd cooked. But today would be different. She stiffened, dreading to see his face when he discovered the empty pot.

"You've stumped me, this time, sweetheart." He leaned closer and sucked in through his nostrils. "I'd guess lima beans, except I've never known you to cook beans without corn bread." Anticipating steam to escape, he picked up a hot pad and slowly lifted the lid.

His laughter caught her by surprise.

With his thumb under her chin, he lifted her face and kissed her. He walked over and opened the door to the cupboard. "Okay, joke's over, funny girl. Where did you hide my lunch?"

"Hide it?" Did he really think . . . She shrugged. "I'm sorry, Coop. Time got away from me, but it won't take long for me to stir something together." She grabbed two potatoes from the bin in the corner and picked up a paring knife. "I'll cut up these potatoes, and an onion and open a can of corned beef to make a pot of hash."

"You're serious? You have nothing cooked?" He rubbed his hand across the back of his neck. "What's wrong? Are you sick?"

How dare he ask if she was sick. Had the date not crossed his mind? Did it not mean anything to him? "I'm fine. I told you time slipped away from me."

Though he was sympathetic the first few months after the miscarriage, his patience had grown thin. Why couldn't he understand? Maybe he could go on as if nothing happened, but she couldn't.

CHAPTER 3

Ludie glared at Schooner, expecting an objection, but when he said, "Line up to kiss the bride," she concluded they had different wedding customs in Georgia. She pleaded for Schooner to rescue her when the three men reeking with the smell of whiskey took turns passing her back and forth as if she were a rag doll.

She screamed, "Please, Schooner! Please, make them stop."

"Okay, boys. You've had your fun. Let her go."

Someone grabbed her from behind and with his arms wrapped around her waist, lifted her up.

Schooner yelled, "I said, that's enough Ox."

"What you talking about? You owe us."

He drew back his fist. "I said let her go. Now!"

"Fine." When he shoved her toward Schooner, Ludie stumbled into her husband's arms, sobbing hysterically.

Ox motioned for his buddy. "Come on, Grander. He can have her. Let's go find us a real woman. One with meat on her bones."

Schooner took his wife by the hand and walked her to his truck. "I'm real sorry 'bout that, little darlin'. I can see they upset you, but no harm done. Right? They were just having a little fun with you."

"Surely, you knew that I wasn't having fun. I thought they were going to . . . to—" She felt a blush rush to her cheeks. "Well, I didn't know what to expect after they begin slobbering all over me. Why didn't you stop them?"

"Aww, shucks, little darlin', they were just funning."

Just as she was about to respond, he pulled up in front of a dilapidated two-story house and stopped.

She looked out the window. "Why are we stopping?"

"This is it."

"It? But it's a rooming house." She pointed to a sign in front of the building.

"Yep!" He opened his door and reached in the bed of the truck for her knapsack.

"I don't understand. You said we'd be living with your folks until you could put a down payment on a place of our own. I suppose your parents own it?"

"Nope."

"What's going on, Schooner?"

"Nothing, sugar foot. I just decided we needed a place to ourselves. You'll love it here." He led her around to the side of the house and pointed to the ramshackle stairs on the side of the building, leading to door, which she assumed had once been a window.

The screen door was hanging on one hinge. He smiled. "You're home."

"Aren't you going to carry me over the threshold?"

"Sure. I forgot that's what husbands do. I ain't never been married before." He scooped her up in his arms, walked inside and tossed her on the bed. He lay down beside her and kissed her on the neck. "I'm really sorry the fellows scared you, hon. Why don't you lay here for a while and get in a few winks before suppertime. Miss Jane is a pretty good cook. I'll be back in time to eat and will wake you up."

"You're leaving?"

"I got a little business to tend to, but I won't be gone long."

"Can't I go with you?"

"Nah, hon. Like I said, it's business.

"What time is supper?"

"Seven o'clock."

"It's almost seven now, Schooner. Do you have to go?"

"That's a silly question. You aren't gonna start nagging on our wedding day, are you? Do you really think I'd leave my brand-new bride if it wasn't important? I'm the only one Daddy will trust to run the business in his absence."

"It feels good to be trusted, doesn't it?" Condemnation washed over her like giant waves splashing against the sand when the tide rushes in. True, she knew how it felt to be trusted; yet, it had taken less than fifteen minutes for the faith the Grahams had placed in

19

her to ebb. "I never quite understood what kind of business you said your father is in."

"Manufacturing and distribution."

"Where's your plant?"

"Plant?" He scratched his head, then arched a brow. "Oh, you mean the location of the business? Just out of town, but the last thing I want to do when I'm with you is to talk shop."

"I'm sorry. I understand, dear. I'll wash up and put on my other dress so I'll be ready when you get back."

"That's my girl."

The words warmed her heart. Ludie walked down the hall to the bathroom smiling and when she returned, she was delighted to see Schooner waiting for her outside the door. "I thought you left. Does this mean you'll be going with—"

He waved her quiet. "I couldn't leave, yet. Ludie, there's something I have to tell you." He stuttered and stammered, and couldn't look her in the eye.

She smiled at how cute he looked. "And what is it you want me to know."

"I want you to know . . . I love you. I really do."

When he grasped her hand in a tight grip, she heard only the sound of her beating heart. "Is that all? Shucks, I knew that already. And I love you, more than you can imagine. I ain't never loved nobody the same way I love you, Schooner Alexander. I feel like I'm the luckiest girl alive."

His eyes twinkled with moisture. "I'll meet you in the dining hall for supper. Maybe ol' lady Jane will make one of her famous pound cakes."

She stood outside their room door and watched as he walked away. He stopped at the top of the stairs, turned around and blew her a kiss. "See you in a bit."

Perhaps it was her imagination, but she sensed there was something troubling her precious husband. Whatever it was, he needed to learn that together, there was nothing they couldn't tackle.

****

Ludie watched the clock and at ten 'til seven she walked downstairs and sat alone in the sitting room, adjacent to the dining hall. A tall, thin, elderly woman with white hair pulled back in a bun, walked over, pushed her spectacles down on her nose, and announced, "If you're here to rent a room, you're in luck. I have one left."

"Oh, we have a room, already."

"Did you say, 'we?'. And what would your room number be?"

"Room Three."

The woman rolled her eyes. "Just as I thought. How many times have I told those boys they can't bring women here. I own a respectable rooming house. Besides, he still owes me."

"Boys? I'm sorry, but it seems you've misunderstood. My husband and I are in Room Three. He was in a hurry to get to the family Plant after we arrived this evening."

The woman's mouth gaped open. "Family Plant? The only

plant that family is familiar with is corn."

Ludie wanted to ask what she meant by such a strange remark, but decided to let it go. She said, "With so much on his mind, I'm sure he merely forgot to pay you. However, he should be here any minute, and will be happy to give you what we owe you." She held out her hand. "I'm Mrs. Schooner Alexander."

The woman held her head back and cackled. "Yeah, and I'm Mrs. Theodore Roosevelt."

"You act as if you don't believe me. Why would I lie?" Not waiting for an answer, her voice quivered. "Perhaps you didn't understand who I said. My husband is—"

"I heard you. Schooner Alexander. But married? That's a laugh. I can't decide if you're trying to make a fool out of me, or if those boys have made one out of you. But regardless of which way it goes, the rent money is still due. I told him when he called to rent the room that if he didn't give me the money when he got here that I'd be locking the door. Honey, if you have belongings in Room Three, I'd advise you to get them out, and then skedaddle as far away from that bunch of hoodlums as you can get. You look like a decent sort of girl. I don't feel sorry for most of the women those boys hang out with, but I hate that he's got a nice girl like you hoodwinked."

There was no reason to argue. She'd wait until Schooner came back and then the old woman could see for herself that she was confusing him with someone else.

After waiting until everyone had left the dining hall and the maid was clearing the table, Ludie decided something serious must've come up to delay Schooner. She went by the kitchen and told Jane that her husband had been detained, but that she had a little money in the room and would get it. She ran out of the kitchen and up the stairs to Room Three. Opening her knapsack, she jerked out all her belongings, searching for the little drawstring change purse. She shook every piece, before spying the tiny bag open on the floor.

After determining it was empty, she trudged down the stairs in an effort to explain to Miss Jane, something that even she couldn't understand. "I must've failed to tighten the string and my money is gone. But Schooner should be here soon, and I'm sure he'll have money to pay you."

The old woman rolled her eyes. "Yep, I have no doubt that he has money and I think we both know what happened to yours."

"No ma'am. You're wrong. He wouldn't have taken mine without telling me. I know he wouldn't. It fell out—it must have."

"Sugar, I won't lock you out this late at night. Try to get a decent night's sleep, and I'll feed you breakfast in the morning. But after that, I expect you to get as far away as possible from Cartersville and that bunch of Alexanders, and don't ever look back."

Ludie ambled up the stairs, holding back the tears until she reached the room, then fell across the bed and wept uncontrollably. "Oh, Schooner, what's going on?" She held to the dwindling hope that there was a plausible explanation, as she cried herself to sleep.

Near midnight, she awoke as Schooner crawled in the bed beside her. "Schooner, where have you been. I've been so worried. You promised to meet me—"

He pressed his finger to her lips. "Shush, pretty baby. Whatever you have to say will wait until tomorrow. He pushed her hair back and kissed her cheek. "We had to move some stuff around at the Plant, and it took more time than I anticipated. But I didn't hurry back to talk about troubles at work. All I could think about was my lovely wife was at home waiting for me."

"But Miss Jane said—"

"Miss Jane?" He popped his palm to his forehead. "Shucks. I meant to pay her before I left. I hope you gave her what we owed."

"I was going to pay her, but my purse was empty. It was open when I found it . . . but the money was gone."

"Holy Smoke! That's right. I'm so sorry, darling. I was counting on you not needing it until I could replace it."

He appeared embarrassed that he had to borrow money from her purse, but she didn't care about the money. Like the apostle Paul, she'd learned to be abased and to abound. Although she couldn't deny having money was a lot more comfortable than not having it, she could make do with very little, as long as they were together.

"I hope you aren't mad. Daddy will pay what he owes me tomorrow. When he does, I'll pay Miss Jane, and replace the money I took from you."

"Shucks, honey, that's not necessary. I'm glad to know I

didn't lose it. Besides, now that we're married, what's mine is yours, and yours is mine." Condemnation made her question if she should confess that for a fleeting moment she had shamefully chosen to believe a woman she'd just met, over her own dear husband. She cringed, recalling the elderly woman's ridiculous accusations. Not that Ludie thought Miss Jane consciously lied, but with men coming in and out of the rooming house on a weekly basis, it was understandable that she confused Schooner with someone else. Of course, that's exactly what happened.

Schooner had made no attempt to lie when she confronted him. He openly admitted he owed the rent money and that he took the money from her purse. Poor, sweet guy. With so much on his mind lately, it was understandable that he could've forgotten to pay Miss Jane.

She threw her arm around him. He picked it up and gently kissed the back of her hand. "I'm sorry it took so long. I'm worn to a frazzle. Goodnight, sweet Ludie." He turned over and went to sleep.

Ludie awoke the next morning and smiled, seeing her handsome husband by her side. Never had she been so conscious of her own body. Her heart thumped erratically.

She'd always wondered what it would feel like to fall in love, and it was even more magnificent than she could've dreamed. Though it wasn't the way she'd imagined her wedding night, she felt blessed beyond measure to be married to such a sweet, hard-working guy. She ran her hand over his muscular arm, and whispered, "Wake-up, my love. It's almost time for breakfast."

He rolled over and pulled something out of his billfold. "Give me your hand."

Ludie stuck out her right hand.

"The other one." He placed a tiny gold band with three little diamond chips on her third finger, left hand. "I told you I'd give you a ring. I wish it could've been bigger, but one day, I'll replace it."

Ludie threw her arms around his neck and all the doubts that had begun to plague her suddenly seemed ridiculous. "Oh, Schooner, it's beautiful. I love it."

After getting dressed, Ludie held her hand in front of her, admiring the ring. "Are you ready to go downstairs?"

"Can't, sweetheart. You need to go without me. I've got business to take care of. I should've left thirty minutes ago.".

"But you have to eat breakfast. Surely, your father would want you to eat, first."

His gaze locked with hers. "Ludie, I know you'd like for us to have our first breakfast together, and so would I. But it's important for you to understand that I have obligations and won't always be there for you when you want me to be. Do you get what I'm saying?"

"Maybe. But what do I tell Miss Jane?"

"About what?"

"The rent money. Do you have it or not?"

"I told you I'd give it to her tonight. Stop worrying. It's my debt. I'll take care of it." He pecked her on the forehead. "Gotta run. See you tonight."

As much as she loved having a ring on her hand, she would've preferred that he pay the rent first, and buy a ring later. Was the old woman right? Was Schooner the loser Miss Jane portrayed him to be? Or had she allowed the old woman's harsh words to poison her thinking?

Four men sat at the breakfast table, and seemed quite content to keep to themselves. Ludie picked up a piece of toast and drank a glass of water, although the pancakes and sausage made her mouth water, and the coffee smelled wonderful. But what right did she have to continue to mount up a bill, which she had no way of paying. After the men finished and left the table, Ludie picked up the dirty dishes and carried them to the kitchen.

Miss Jane walked in and reminded her that the boarders weren't required to wash dishes.

"I'd like to talk to you about what I owe. I want to pay you for the room and meals, but since my money is gone, I have no other way to pay you, other than to work off the debt. I promise in time, I will pay whatever you feel I owe."

"Honey, come on back in the dining room and sit down. You and I need to have a little talk."

Ludie's stomach churned. Was she in trouble? What if the woman called the law and had her arrested?

Jane came walking in with two fresh hot cups of coffee and sat one down in front of her.

"No thank you. I can't keep imposing on your generosity."

"Shucks, child, no imposition at all. Now, let's talk about what you're doing here."

Just as she thought. It would only be a matter of time before she'd be locked up in the Hoosegow. What would Gracie and Garth think if they should find out? Ludie knew exactly what they'd think, and they'd be right to judge her harshly.

Miss Jane said, "Do you take cream and sugar?"

"Got no right, ma'am."

"We don't drink coffee because we've secured the right. We drink it because it gets our day off to a good start. Now, do you use cream and sugar?"

Ludie smiled. "Yes ma'am." She prepared her coffee, then sipped slowly. "It's good. Real good. Thank you, Miss Jane."

"Honey, what made you take up with those Alexanders?"

"I don't know why you keep referring to my husband as if he came in a package deal. I don't know any of his folks. We just got married yesterday, so I haven't met any of his family."

"Do you mind telling me where you got married?"

"No ma'am, although I ain't proud of it. We married back of a storefront."

"Really? Here in Cartersville?"

"Yes'm. Actually, it's a bar, called Bottoms Up, but there's a room in the back where weddings take place. You ever heard of it?"

Jane chewed the inside of her cheek, then nodded. "I know about Bottoms Up, but I've never heard of weddings being held in a back room there."

"Oh, yes'm. That's where we got married."

"I see. And who married you, sweetheart?"

"A young preacher named Brother Brute. Being this is a small town, I reckon you've heard of him."

"Oh, sugar, I hate to tell you, but you aren't married."

Just as Ludie had begun to like Miss Jane, the woman practically called her a liar. "Yes ma'am, I most certainly am married. Just because you ain't never heard of the preacher or didn't know about the chapel back of the bar, that don't mean it didn't take place."

Miss Jane's eyes squinted. "Sugar, what did you tell me your name is?"

"I'm Mrs. Schooner Alexander. My name is Eliza Clementine, though most folks call me Ludie."

"Well, Ludie, I have some news for you that you won't like, but someone has to tell you. Honey, Brute, Ox and Grander are all Schooner Alexander's brothers."

She swallowed hard. "No. That can't be. He would've told me."

"Not if he wanted to bamboozle you into thinking you were married. Brute has probably never stepped foot inside of a church, and he's certainly no preacher. He works in the bar during the day, and they all run their Daddy's moonshine still at night. A sorrier bunch of fellows would be hard to find."

Ludie's breath came out in short, heavy pants. "You mean . . .are you sure . . .sure I ain't married?"

"I'm quite sure. I've known those boys all their lives, and they're always up to no-good."

"This can't be true. Last night I—" She burst into sobs.

Miss Jane's chin quivered. "Oh, honey, what a dirty trick they played on you. Criminal, if you ask me. The town would be better off if the law would send them all off to work on the chain gang. It would be the only honest work any of them have ever done."

Ludie dried her eyes, slid her chair back and stood. "Thank you, Miss Jane, for being truthful with me. She reached down and picked up her knapsack from off the floor. I promise you, I'll pay you what I owe, as soon as I get the money."

"Honey, you owe me nothing. Schooner owes me, and I'll see that he pays. I guarantee you, he'll pay! Where are you from, Ludie?"

"Lower Alabama. A little place called Goat Hill, Alabama. I don't reckon you've ever heard of it, but it's down near the Florida line."

"Well, I suppose you'll be going back home. Go in the kitchen, look in the pantry and get whatever you need for the journey and don't worry about paying. As I said, I'll collect from the one who owes me. Now, go get what you need, and I'll be upstairs changing linens on the beds if you should need me before you leave."

Ludie felt the right thing to do would be to turn down the offer. However, after mulling it over and knowing Schooner would be charged, it made it easier to do as Miss Jane suggested and get what she might need to survive. She took one tin plate, cup, fork, knife, three apples, two cans of sardines, a sleeve of soda crackers and a wedge of cheese. Stuffing them into her knapsack, she felt as if she were stealing, although Miss Jane had insisted. Looking into the bag, she pulled out an apple. It didn't seem right to take three.

She threw her knapsack over her back and walked out the door and down the street, with no destination in mind. The only place she didn't want to be was in town where Schooner might find her. Even if she had the money for a bus ticket home, she was too ashamed to go back and face Garth and Gracie. She'd walked seven or eight miles down a long dusty road, when a car load of loud hoodlums pulled up beside her. When they first stopped, she thought it was Schooner and his brothers. After she refused to talk to them, they finally pulled off and left her alone. Grateful that it wasn't the Alexander brothers, she realized it wasn't smart to be walking where she could be easily spotted. If she never saw Schooner again, it would be too soon.

How could he have stooped so low? She shivered thinking about him crawling into her bed, after tricking her into believing they were married. The only thing Brute got right in the ceremony was when he called it "awfully married." Nothing could have been more awful, and she and Schooner were definitely not lawfully married. Never would she be able to live down the shame.

A truck loaded with squawking chickens whizzed by. Spotting dense woods to her left, she decided to avoid the road and walk in that direction, where no one would be likely to see her. Not ever having been to Cartersville, she had no idea what might lie on the other side of the thick swamps, but did it matter? As long as Schooner couldn't find her, one place would be as good as the next.

The woods were much thicker than she had imagined. She'd begun to wonder if there was an end to them when she came upon a river. It was too wide to cross, but she was tired, her feet hurt, and the water looked inviting. With no one around, she laid down her bag, pulled off her clothes and jumped in.

After a reinvigorating swim, she got out, dressed and decided it was as good a place as any to set up camp. Perhaps tomorrow she'd have a clearer understanding of where she was to go from there.

CHAPTER 4

Cooper Flanigan grabbed his hat from off the nail and stomped toward the door. "Forget it, Carly. I don't have time to wait. This is the second time this week that I've come home to find you haven't made lunch."

"I'm sorry. Time slipped away from me. Sit down and I'll make you a sandwich in a hurry. I bought a few bananas yesterday." She jerked open the cabinet door, then groaned. "Oh, dear, I meant to buy bananas. I guess I forgot. What if I fix you—"

He shoved his chair back when he stood, and it fell to the floor. He sat it back up and grunted. "I don't have time to wait for you to fix lunch. The guys will be at the site shortly to lay the brick." He glanced toward the sink at the dirty breakfast dishes. "What have you been doing all morning, Carly? Have you even fed Emma? He looked around. "Where is she?"

"Emma?"

"Yes. You do remember we have a daughter, don't you?"

Such an absurd statement didn't require a response, though she mumbled, "She's playing out back. I'll call her in."

"No, let her play. I'm sure she's happy it finally stopped raining so she could go outside."

Would he think her a bad mother if she admitted she had allowed Emma to play outside all week, even on the rainy days? Though Emma was the daughter of Coop's deceased sister, Carly had considered the child to be theirs, even before the adoption went through.

Cooper grabbed an apple and stomped out of the house.

Surely, he blamed her for the baby's death, and rightly so. Hadn't he scolded her more than once during her pregnancy for climbing on the ladder? If only she'd listened. The guilt ate away at her like a fast-growing cancer. When they first began to talk of building a new house near the river, she could hardly wait. The nursery would be painted yellow and would face the west end, so the rising sun wouldn't wake the sleeping infant at daybreak. But since the accident, she hadn't cared if the house was ever finished. She didn't care about anything, anymore.

After everything she'd been through in her life, losing the baby was the hardest. Some things were out of her control, but not this. Was it her fault that her first husband, Julian, died after the sawmill accident? Of course not. Nor was it her fault that her second husband, sweet J.C. lost his life by being on the wrong train at the wrong time. And there was no way she could be blamed for being kidnapped by a crazed bus driver. But climbing on a rickety old ladder two months before the baby's due date was preventable. No wonder Coop could barely stand to look at her.

Emma came running through the back door, yelling, "Mommy, I'm hungry. When is Daddy coming home for lunch?"

"He's already come and gone, sweetheart."

"Why didn't you call me?"

"He was in a hurry. Would you like a bowl of cereal?"

She turned up her nose. "I had cereal for breakfast."

Carly's lip quivered. The child was right. "Uh, would you like a peanut butter sandwich?"

"And chocolate milk?"

Carly nodded. "And chocolate milk. Have a seat at the table and I'll have it ready, shortly."

Her mind raced back to the first time she met this precious little girl. Coop had accepted the responsibility of raising his sister's orphaned child and he was doing a great job of it. Much better than she'd been doing lately. It wasn't as if she wanted to linger in a state of despair. How many times in the past had she vowed to heed the advice by well-meaning friends, to 'get over it." But how does one get over losing a child, especially when the burden of guilt is indisputable?

Emma finished her lunch and asked for a syrup bucket to use for catching top minnows at the river. With her mind preoccupied, Carly reached up and took a bucket from the top shelf in the pantry and handed to the child.

Emma babbled something, then ran out the door. Carly pushed

herself to go to the turnip patch to cut a mess of greens for supper. She'd cook a few slices of fat-back, bake some sweet potatoes and corn pones, and after a hearty supper, maybe Coop would forgive her for not having his lunch ready.

Later that day, she was washing the turnips when Coop ran through the door with Emma in his arms.

"Call the doctor. Quick!"

"What's wrong with Emma, and why is she wet??"

He screamed, "I said call the doctor."

Carly made the call, though all she could relate to Doctor Mitchell was that it was an emergency. Cooper sat at the table, cradling the child in his arms, his lips planted on her forehead.

"What happened, Coop? She's not . . . she's not—"

"Dead? No, but she would've been if that girl hadn't been there."

"What girl?" She reached for the child, but Cooper ignored her and held little Emma close to his chest.

"Please tell me what happened. She's gonna be alright, isn't she?"

Before he could answer, the doctor rushed through the door. "What's the problem?"

Cooper said, "She fell in the river and was being carried out with the current, when a young woman saw her, jumped in and pulled her out. She wasn't breathing when the girl brought her to me. I thought for sure we'd lost her. I got her breathing, but she keeps going in and out of consciousness. Even when she's conscious, she just looks at me, then closes her eyes and appears to be gone again."

"How long was she in the water?"

"I have no idea. I wasn't there. I was working on the new house."

The doctor glanced at Carly with a raised brow.

She lowered her head. "I wasn't there, either."

Cooper said, "Emma knows we don't allow her to go to the river alone. She's never slipped off before."

"I see. Please lay her on the bed and let me take a look." He shut the door behind him. After what seemed an eternity, the doctor walked back out and said, "That river can be mean. Your little girl is very lucky to be alive. I'd advise you to keep a closer watch on her from now on."

Cooper looked at Carly and though he didn't mouth the words, she was certain what he was thinking: *It's my wife's fault. I was at work.* And of course, he'd be right. She'd killed their baby boy and because of her negligence, they'd almost lost sweet little Emma. She clasped her lips tightly to keep the screams from escaping.

The ornery old doctor seemed to think it his responsibility to dispense a strong rebuke along with his medical advice. "I can't for the life of me understand why you'd build a house even closer to the river, when you know you have a strong-willed child, who doesn't do as she's told. I've given her a sedative and she'll likely sleep until morning. But if you ask me, as soon as she's better, that young'un needs a switching on those little legs that she won't soon forget."

The doctor left and Carly finished putting supper on the table. She waited for Coop to say something. Anything. The silence was killing her.

He sat down and picked up a corn pone. After two bites, he laid it on his plate. "Sorry, I can't eat."

"But you didn't eat lunch. You need something."

His eyes glared. "You're right, Carly. I do need something, but it's not on the table."

Hurt, she assumed he meant the food she prepared was not to his liking. She grabbed the bowl of turnips, the meat, potatoes, and bread and raked it all in the slop jar for the pigs.

Sliding his chair back, he stood and threw his napkin on the table. "I'm exhausted. I plan to sleep in Emma's room to keep check on her. Good night."

Carly pumped water in the sink to wash the dishes. Was Cooper blaming her for Emma going to the river? Though she had resented the doctor's rebuke, perhaps he had a point. Emma had been told repeatedly not to go to the river alone, yet she chose to slip away. But strong-willed?

Carly dried the aluminum pot and put it on the top shelf in the pantry beside three empty syrup buckets. But weren't there four? She shoved pans around on the shelf, searching for the missing bucket. Her heart sank. Only then, did she recall pulling one down and handing to Emma. "Why would she ask for a—" Swallowing the lump in her throat, she vaguely recalled her saying something about top minnows? Carly clasped her hand over her mouth. What had she done? *Cooper will never forgive me if he discovers that Emma not only told me of her plan, I handed her a pail and sent her on the way.*

Just as the doctor predicted, Emma slept through the night, and awoke in a cheerful mood.

She chirped away at the breakfast table, as if nothing had happened. "Mama, I wanna go to the river and find the girl who lives in the swamp."

Coop's lip curled. "Young lady, I would think you would've learned your lesson. I hope I never hear of you going to the river alone, again. Do you understand?"

"But I have to find her, Daddy. She's my friend. I slipped and fell in the water and she pushed me up so I could breathe."

Carly said, "Coop, I thought we knew everyone within miles. I wonder who she is."

"Beats me. I'd never seen her before, but I thank the Lord that she was in the right place at the right time. My heart stopped when I saw her running toward me holding Emma, soaking wet and as limp as a ragdoll. Of course, assumed the worse."

"Did she not tell you her name?"

"No, I didn't take time to ask questions. Every minute was precious. All I know is that she was an angel for risking her own life. The water was rough."

"I wish we knew where she lives so we could compensate her

some way for being so brave."

Emma said, "She doesn't live in a house. She lives in the swamp."

Carly's lip curled. "Does she, dear?"

"You don't believe me, but she really does."

Carly breathed easier, seeing Coop's smile. Perhaps she only imagined that he blamed her for the accident. Naturally, he was upset that they could've lost their precious Emma. If only she could dismiss the haunting memory of Emma running out of the house, holding the syrup bucket—the bucket she'd given her.

He pecked Carly on the cheek before leaving, although she assumed it to be out of a sense of duty and not a guarantee that she was forgiven.

When Coop came home for lunch, Carly was ready for him.

He walked over and threw the mail on the table, then pumped water into the sink and washed his hands. Sucking in through his nostrils, he let out a pleasant moan. "Country fried steak!" Lifting the lid, he smiled. "Thanks, hon. Smells wonderful. My favorite."

She sat a bowl of creamed potatoes, gravy, green beans, poke salat and biscuits on the table. Consumed by grief, she had neglected the two people who meant more to her than anything on earth. Though losing the baby caused her stomach to wrench every time she thought about it, which was practically every minute of every day, she still had much to be thankful.

Cooper had almost finished his lunch, when he said, "Oh, I

almost forgot. You have a letter."

Carly thumbed through the envelopes, when her eyes focused on a post mark from Marl, Alabama. She laid the envelopes back on the table without opening.

"Well?"

"What?"

"Aren't you going to read it?"

"No."

His brow creased. "Why not?"

"Did you see the postmark?"

"I did. I assume it's from Pearl."

"And that's exactly why I'm not going to read it. Besides, it's addressed to Mrs. Carly Thornbury. I'm Mrs. Cooper Flannigan, and she knows it, although I'm sure it would pain her to admit it."

Cooper through up his hands. "My lands, sweetheart, you can't hold onto that grudge forever."

"Can't I?"

"It's wrong and you know it. Unforgiveness will hurt you much more than it will Pearl. Sure, she's high strung, selfish, and yes, even manipulative at times—but I've found it in my heart to forgive her for wronging us, and I think you should, too."

"How considerate of you, Coop, but don't expect me to forget how she tried to come between us." Carly bristled. Hadn't she had enough to deal with lately? Losing the baby and knowing it was her fault, Coop's lack of understanding, then almost losing Emma due to her negligence was more than she could take. The last thing on earth she needed was for Pearl Greene to make her way back into their lives. Why now? Could their marriage withstand any more testing?

"If you aren't going to open it, Carly, then I will. I'm a little disappointed that you choose to harbor such ill will toward someone who was once our dear friend."

Her eyes widened. "*Our* friend? Are you serious? She was never my friend, although she put on a good act in an effort to get you."

"But she didn't get me, now did she? So what are you worried about?"

"Because she's like a magician. She has more tricks in her bag, and she'll try them all. She used me and Julian to get you from Cartersville to Marl, by promising we could stay with her until we could build a house. But once we got you there, she lied and left us to fend for ourselves. I blame her for Julian's death."

"Honey, I'll admit, in the past Pearl wasn't always truthful and was underhanded in some of her dealings, but Julian died of gangrene. There was no way Pearl could be blamed for that."

"How can you sit there and defend her, when you know she turned us out of her home when we arrived, and Julian was in need of immediate medical attention?"

"She could've been more cordial, but Julian would've still died, even if she had." He picked up the letter, opened it and read aloud.

"Dear Carly,

It is with a broken heart I pen this letter. My darling Ed died from a heart attack and I feel so lost without him. I plan to sell the store and relocate. I can't bear to stay in Marl, since I blame the move here to be responsible for my dear husband's death. I loved him with all my heart, but the store demanded so much of his time, and left me feeling left out of his life.

Though circumstances caused us to drift apart for a while, I realize Ed never stopped loving me, nor I him. I am so distraught over his demise. Therefore, I've decided to move back to Cartersville, where we shared our happiest memories. We never sold our house there, and even though I'm sure it will take a lot of work, it will be wonderful having you as a neighbor, once again. I trust Cooper and sweet little Emma are doing well. I can hardly wait to see them, and you, of course. However, I must wait until I find a buyer for the house and store, but I trust it won't take long.

Carly, I won't deny things were strained between us when we last met, but I pray that's all buried in the past, for I remain,

Your dear friend,

Pearl Greene"

Cooper folded the letter and stuck it back in the envelope. "I hate to hear that."

Carly rolled her eyes. "Not nearly as bad as I hate to hear it. She'll never give up on you, Coop."

"Oh, Carly! I meant I hated to hear about Ed. He was a good man. She didn't mention the boys."

"Are you surprised? Her kids were never a priority. I couldn't believe she could walk out on them, leaving Ed to take care of them alone. I still can't understand how she could've deserted them, or Ed. He was a sweet man, but if ever I've seen a hen-pecked husband, he was one, for sure. I felt sorry for him, getting tangled up with such a cold-hearted woman."

"Honey, we don't always know what someone else is going through. But you need to let go of the animosity. Pearl will be our neighbor and it's evident from her letter that she's heartbroken over the loss of her husband. You don't have to become bosom buddies, but I do think we need to treat her with the compassion and respect we'd have for any grieving widow when she arrives."

"Like the respect and compassion, which she showed me? She made me a widow by turning us away when Julian was so ill."

"Carly, this cold-heartedness doesn't become you. I hope you'll have a change of attitude when she becomes our neighbor."

Biting the inside of her cheek, she mumbled, "I think you can count on it. I feel a definite attitude change already, just knowing she'll be living down the road."

"I need to get back. The guys slack up when I leave them alone, and I'm counting on having the house finished by next month." He stood and pecked her on the forehead. "I'm sorry if I upset you. I know you'll do the right thing when the time comes. No sense in attempting to solve problems before they exist. Besides, she said she must sell the house and store, first, and who knows how long that might take?"

After he left, Carly gave thought to her husband's words. He expected her to do "the right thing," as he put it. She understood the meaning behind his words to imply the right thing would be to welcome Pearl with open arms as if nothing had ever happened. How dare he expect her to forgive and forget all the wrongs pitted against her by that vicious woman. If he thought that would ever happen, he had a new thought coming. Pearl Greene's excuse for moving back to Cartersville hadn't fooled her for a minute and if Cooper thought this conversation was over, he was dead wrong.

An enlightening thought flashed in her head, exposing Pearl's devious plan and leaving Carly gasping that she could've been so naïve. Pearl would choose to play the martyr, taking advantage of Cooper's soft heart, while attempting to portray Carly as spiteful and unforgiving, thus driving a wedge between her and her husband. It couldn't be plainer. The longer Carly thought about it, the more she realized it was imperative that she come up with her own battle plan.

A wry smile crossed her lips when it became clear what she must do. She'd shower Pearl with such an overwhelming abundance of pseudo affection that if it were possible for so much sweetness to cast the recipient into a diabetic coma, Pearl would be immobilized. Carly snickered. Pearl would be furious when she realized she was being beat by her own game, and her true dark colors would be exposed. Coop would be so proud of his precious wife for trying so sweetly to mend the relationship with their dear friend, and the blame for the broken ties would land squarely on Pearl's shoulders. It wouldn't be easy, but the outcome would be worth the effort. The quicker she could send Pearl back to Marl, the happier she'd be.

Her thoughts were interrupted when Emma ran into the room and jerked on her skirt. "Come see who's here, Mommy. Quick!"

CHAPTER 5

Emma tugged on Carly's hand, pulling her toward the back door. Only one person could stir such excitement in the child. Her *Aunt* Pearl, as Pearl insisted she call her. Carly's teeth ground together. All sorts of thoughts flashed through her mind.

Pearl had used Emma to try to get to Cooper in the past and it almost worked. Sucking in a lungful of air, she had to stay focused. Though it wouldn't be easy, she had a plan and she had to stick with it. Her hand trembled as she pushed open the back door. Could she really throw her arms around Pearl Greene, as if nothing had ever happened? Did she have a choice?

Emma pointed to a ragged-looking urchin standing there, mumbling incoherently. Hobos often showed up asking to work for food, but this was neither Pearl nor the usual hobo. The poor girl never once looked Carly in the face, but kept her head lowered.

Carly said, "What is it you want? You'll have to speak up,

girl."

The young woman lifted her eyes, slightly, then shook her head, turned and ran into the woods.

Emma screamed, "Come back. Please come back," then burst into tears.

Carly knelt down beside her. "Honey, I think she came to the wrong house and was embarrassed. You mustn't cry. I wonder who she is."

"She's the Swamp Angel."

Carly recalled seeing one of Emma's comic books about a Swamp Creature that bore a rather gruesome-looking cover. She had warned Coop that he needed to be more observant of the books the child picked out when accompanying him to the drug store. Though Emma referred to them as "funny books," there was nothing funny about some of these covers, which could cause an adult to have nightmares. "Honey, there is no such thing as a Swamp . . .whatever you called her. Do you see what happens when you read about frightening characters in those comic books? You begin to believe they're real."

"But she is real. Daddy called her an angel, and she lives in the swamp."

"Did your father read the book to you?"

"You don't believe me, do you? She pulled me out of the river and handed me to daddy."

Carly's heart sank. "You mean that was her? Oh, my word, I'm so sorry, sugar. I wish I had known. I wonder why she didn't say something."

Emma frowned. "She did."

"She mumbled something, but surely she was aware I didn't understand her."

"I understood. She said, "Hungry, hungry.""

"Did she? Poor girl. Well, I'm sorry I didn't know. If she comes back, please encourage her to stay until I can fix her something to eat. It's the least we can do to show our appreciation. I wonder where she lives."

"I told you—"

Seeing Emma's dropped jaw, she quickly added, "I meant I wonder where in the swamps she lives, sweetheart."

Carly found it difficult to get her mind off the image of that pitiful looking ragamuffin, shifting from one foot to the other, looking like a little scared rabbit. It wouldn't be hard to believe the poor creature might be hungry. But who was she and where did she live? She ran in the direction of the river, yet there were no houses in the woods. The closest house was the one owned by Pearl, a good half-mile down the road.

Carly cut up a chicken for supper, but she couldn't get her mind off the girl. After putting the chicken in the Frigidaire, she washed her hands and called for Emma. "Why don't we walk over to where your daddy and the fellows are working on our new house?"

Emma seemed pleased to be taking a walk. "I'll pick some

flowers to go on the supper table. There are lots of flowers near our new house."

"That's a great idea, honey. They're called Goldenrod and they make some people sneeze."

Emma's big blue eyes twinkled. "That's funny. Kerchoo! Kerchoo." She giggled as she faked one sneeze after another.

Cooper laid down the hammer and met them halfway as soon as he spotted them. With a hand shielding the sun from his eyes, he gazed at the house and said, "So, what do you think?"

"About what?"

A feeling of shock shot through him like a bolt of lightning. "The house, of course."

"Oh. It looks fine."

Fine? *Fine?* Was that all she could say? His thoughts trailed back to the day they first walked over the level plot of ground to plan their dream home. Carly stood in the spot where the kitchen would be. Then, pretending to be washing dishes in the sink, she gazed out the make-believe window and talked about seeing the children playing tag. *Children.* She didn't say she saw Emma . . . but she was seeing children.

He recalled how she grabbed him around the waist, and exclaimed, "Oh, Coop, I'm so excited. I can hardly wait for you to begin building. It's gonna be a beautiful house." She insisted the nursery be painted yellow, since it would be an appropriate color, regardless of the sex of the baby. "If it's yellow, we won't need to repaint every time I get pregnant."

Then she became pregnant, and they decorated a room in the old house. But when the baby died, the dream inside Carly died with him. Cooper decided to wait for her to get through the grief period before starting to build, but after waiting for over two years, he concluded she wasn't trying to move on. She never talked of getting pregnant again and when he tried to bring up the subject, she'd go into a crying frenzy, accusing him of not caring that she'd lost the baby. Why couldn't she realize it was his baby, too? He blinked away the tears. No man had ever wanted a son as much as he, but for Emma's sake, as well as for their marriage, wasn't it time to get on with their lives?

"Cooper? What's wrong?"

His voice cracked. "I'd hoped you'd show a little more enthusiasm, Carly."

"My goodness, who put a burr in your saddle? It's plain to see that you and the fellows have worked very hard, and it's coming along nicely. But I didn't come to discuss the house. We had an unexpected visitor today and in case she shows up again, I need to know what you think we should do."

His brow meshed together. "Good grief, Carly. I hope you didn't come here to discuss Pearl, because I don't have time for that conversation."

"Not Pearl. It was the young woman who rescued Emma from the river."

Feeling guilty for allowing his imagination to carry him to

such a dark place, he considered apologizing. But since the bitter feelings had remained inward and not uttered aloud, he decided it best to let it go, rather than to bring up a sore subject. "So, what did the girl want?"

"I'm not sure, but I think she wanted food."

"Well, I hope you fed her well. If not for her, we would've lost Emma."

"That's the thing. I had no idea who she was, nor could I understand her. She mumbled something, then ran away before I could find out what she wanted. It was after she left that Emma told me who she was and that she understood her to say she was hungry."

"Then we have to find her."

"I agree. Why don't you ask the fellows working on the house if any of them might know her? I can't imagine where she might live."

Emma held tightly to a handful of goldenrod. "I know where she lives."

Cooper said, "Where, honey?"

Carly smiled and winked. "Emma thinks she lives in the swamp."

Emma's brow shot up. "I know she lives there. She told me so." Spotting a pile of sand near the new house, she handed the flowers to Carly, and ran to play in the sand.

Cooper said, "There's no way she could've told Emma anything, since Emma was not even conscious when the girl handed her to me. I'm concerned about Em's growing imagination. I've begun to agree with you that her obsession with comic books is affecting her ability to separate fact from fiction. It's cute at this age, how she can become totally lost in her imaginary world, but it could spell trouble down the road, if we don't start insisting that she always tell the truth and cease with these outlandish fantasies."

Carly nodded as if she understood, though she wasn't totally sure that she did. "But she seems so sure, Coop. What if . . . I'm not saying I'm convinced, but what if the girl did tell her that she lives in the swamp?"

"Don't take up for her, sweetheart. We've done that too many times. I told her the story last week about the little boy who cried wolf. I was hoping it would register with her, but apparently it didn't."

"But how do you know that this time she's not telling—"

"The truth?" He rolled his eyes. "For one thing, Emma wasn't breathing when the girl laid her in my arms. If the girl had told her anything, she wouldn't have heard her, since she was unconscious. The girl stood speechless until I pumped air back into her lungs, and then she ran off before I had time to thank her. If that's not proof enough, I don't know how much plainer it could be."

"I suppose you're right. I'll speak with Emma and let her know we don't approve of such behavior."

Cooper glanced toward the house. "The guys seem to be slacking off. I'd better get back and keep the hammer swinging or we won't be settled in by Thanksgiving."

Emma pleaded to stay and play in the sand, and Cooper assured Carly she'd be fine.

"But it's so close to the river. You don't think—?"

"Hon, we've gone over this before. The river will always be in view, but I can assure you, she's learned her lesson. I want her to always have a healthy fear of the danger, but not so terrified of the water that she'll never be able to enjoy the pleasures it shall bring us. And when we have more chil—"

Carly turned sharp and yelled for Emma. Cooper got the message. She had no intention of discussing the possibility.

Carly held the goldenrod in her hand and reached up in the cabinet for a vase when someone knocked on the door. Afraid the young woman had come back and would leave if she didn't hurry, she rushed to open the door. She dropped the flowers and tried to collect her thoughts. "Pearl?"

She snickered. "Yes, Carly, it's me. Do I look so different you didn't recognize me?" She reached up and patted her new coif. "It must be my new hairstyle?"

"Oh, I recognize you. I was just surprised to see you."

Pearl reached down, picked up the flowers and handed them to Carly, smiling. "Didn't you get my letter?"

"Yes, but I didn't expect you so soon, since you said you had to sell the house and store before moving."

"And I do." She nodded toward the flowers. "Shouldn't you put those in water? I suppose my sweet Emma picked them. I only came to check out our old house, and to find someone to do the needed repairs before I move in. Ed was no carpenter and I'm afraid it was in disrepair before we moved to Marl, so I'm sure there's much to be done." She cocked her head as if to look past Carly. "Where is my sweet little Emma. Please tell her Aunt Pearl is here. I can't begin to tell you how much I've missed that precious child."

How dare she keep referring to Emma as her little Emma. "I'm afraid she isn't here, Pearl."

"I see. Well, I hope she won't be gone long." Then smiling, she said, "Do you intend to invite me in, or are you still holding a grudge? I've missed you, Carly."

Carly felt oddly paralyzed. She'd almost forgotten her plan. "Of course, you're welcome here. Please pardon my manners. Won't you come in?" She thought of inviting her to stay for supper, which would surely give Coop the impression she was the sweet, forgiving wife, although she had every right to scratch the conniving woman's eyeballs out.

Pearl made a point to take in every inch of the room as her eyes darted from one corner to the next. "I'm sure it was difficult for Cooper to leave his beautiful family home and come here to this little farmhouse. . . not that it isn't cozy, but he was brought up differently. And how is your handsome husband?"

Carly smiled through her teeth. "He's wonderful. And he says he'd be happy anywhere, as long as we're together." She swallowed hard, realizing she was slipping away from being the loving friend she'd wished to portray. "I'd be pleased if you'd stay for supper, but of course, I realize you didn't come this far to visit, so if you need to take care of business, I'll understand."

The front door opened, and Emma squealed. "Daddy said that's Aunt Pearl's car in the yard. Where is she?"

Pearl stooped down with open arms. "Here, I am, my precious Emma." Hugging her tightly, tears fell from her eyes. "Your Aunt Pearl has missed you so much, darling. Have you missed me?"

She nodded, then stood erect with her shoulders held back. "See how big I am?"

"Yes, you are. You must've grown several inches since I last saw you. I never had a little girl of my own, so I've always wanted to pretend you were mine."

Carly stiffened.

Pearl's eyes lit up when she looked up at Cooper. Then standing with open arms, she gushed, "Well, hello, Cooper. Surprised to see me?"

Coop glanced at his wife, sheepishly. "Yes, a little. We weren't expecting you so soon, were we dear?" He bent down and kissed his wife.

"No, but our home is always open to our—"

Pearl didn't appear interested in Carly's response. She eyed Cooper from head to toe and said, "Well, you're even better looking than when I last saw you. Don't stand there like a scarecrow. Don't I get a hug?"

He rubbed his hand across the back of his neck and shot a glance toward his wife. "Uh, of course." He placed an arm on

Pearl's shoulder and gave a quick little pat on the back.

Pearl threw her arms around his neck. "What kind of hug is that?" With only a nose-length between them, she gazed into his eyes, with the fascination a new calf has when looking at a new gate. "You look great, Coop." She slid a hand down and pressed it against his bicep and swooned. "Hard work becomes you. I've missed you so . . . uh, you and Carly, both, of course. It will be good having my best friends as neighbors once again."

Coop pushed away, then walked over and stood beside his wife.

Though she'd rather be walking on a bed of nails, Carly had no intention of giving Pearl the satisfaction of knowing she was jealous. Wrapping her arm around her husband's waist, her lip quivered when she feigned a smile. "Darling, I told Pearl we would be delighted if she'd stay for supper. I'm afraid it's nothing fancy, since I wasn't expecting company. But if she likes fried chicken and biscuits, we're more than glad to share what we have."

Cooper looked at her as if he wondered if the words were coming from her mouth.

Pearl said, "You can imagine my answer, Coop. He can attest to the fact that I love fried chicken and biscuits. Of all the meals I carried to him while he lived in Marl, it was my favorite and also the one he most requested."

This was beginning to get much harder that Carly could've imagined, but she had to keep her focus and not allow Pearl to get the upper hand. It was easy to see that Coop was uncomfortable, not knowing what to expect from her. Well, he was in for the surprise of his life.

Pearl said, "Emma, I almost forgot. Aunt Pearl brought you a surprise. It's on the front seat of my automobile. Why don't you go get it and bring it in the house to open it?"

Emma threw her arms around her. "A present? For me?"

"Yes, dear. I hope you like it."

Emma came running back in the house holding a box almost as long as she was tall. She sat it on the floor and tore off the paper. Squealing with delight, she screamed, "Look, Mommy. Isn't this the most beautiful doll in the whole wide world? And she's almost as big as me. Thank you, Aunt Pearl."

Cooper glanced at Carly. "Pearl, I don't think you should have—"

Carly reached for his hand, "What Coop means is that it was too generous of you, but awfully sweet. She loves it. Thank you."

Cooper's brow creased. "Uh, yes. I agree with Carly. It was very generous of you. Thank you."

Carly said, "Well, the biscuits are done, so shall we all get to the table?"

Cooper picked up the platter of chicken and handed to Pearl.

"Thank you." After taking a bite, she said, "Carly, have you ever tried dipping the chicken in buttermilk before flouring? I think you'll find it makes them much crispier. Cooper always loved the crusty coating on my chicken, didn't you Coop?"

His Adam's apple bobbed. "Yes, but I also love my wife's

chicken."

Carly smiled, but this time it wasn't fake. Her plot was working. "Oh, honey, thank you, but it's awfully sweet of Pearl to share her cooking tips. I'm sure she's a terrific cook. Pearl, why don't you and Coop go sit by the fire and catch up on the news, while I clean the kitchen?"

"Thank you, I think we shall. I've always coveted Cooper's advice. I am facing some decisions that could affect my future, and I'd love to get his opinion."

Cooper said, "Carly and I do the supper dishes together. It won't take long. Please make yourself at home in the front room by the fire, Pearl, and we'll be in there shortly."

"*You* wash dishes?" She gave a sarcastic chuckle. "I'm shocked. Why, Ed Greene never washed a dish in his life. I suppose I'm old-fashioned, but I always felt kitchen duties were my responsibility. We're all different, I suppose. Oh, well . . . it's getting late, so I suppose I should go. I plan to stay in the Cartersville hotel for a couple of days, so maybe tomorrow you can spare me a few minutes of your time? Being a widow is dreadfully hard." She managed to squeeze a tear or two from her left tear duct. "There are so many decisions facing me that I never had to make before and it's very distressful."

"I'm sorry."

"Oh, I wasn't seeking sympathy. Just stating a fact of life. I don't intend to unleash all my troubles on you, but I trust you to help guide me in making the right decisions."

"I'll do what I can, Pearl."

"I passed by your new house earlier. It's quite beautiful, but I'd expect no less from you. Perhaps I could meet you there, tomorrow. What time would be good for you?"

Carly said, "Goodness, I hope you aren't planning on rushing off. There'll be plenty of time for you to ask Cooper all sorts of questions after we finish in the kitchen. We insist you spend the night here if you don't mind sleeping with Emma." She looked at her husband, "Isn't that right, dear?"

The way his head made a slight sweeping motion, it was difficult to tell if his response was in the affirmative or negative.

The fervor with which Pearl shook her head, left no doubt that this didn't fit in with her plans. "That's awfully sweet of you to offer, Carly, but I wouldn't think of imposing. I'm sure poor Cooper is tired. It'll be no problem for me to meet him tomorrow at the job site."

"Oh, no you won't. We wouldn't hear of it. There's no need for you to stay in a hotel and I think you'll be very comfortable in Emma's room. For sure, she'll be thrilled to have her Aunt Pearl sleeping with her. Give us ten or fifteen minutes in the kitchen and we'll join you, shortly. Cooper and I never go to bed this early, so we'll be prepared to stay up as long as you have questions."

"You're very thoughtful, Carly, but as much as I'd love to sit up and talk with my two best friends, I'm bushed. Would you be terribly offended if I decline your offer to spend the night?"

"Not at all. Coop comes home for lunch at 11:30 every day.

Since that's the only break he'll have, please agree to have lunch with us. If he doesn't have time to finish answering your questions, we'll insist you join us for supper." Carly glanced at her husband's bewildered looking face and wondered if she might be overdoing it. But she could read Pearl Greene like a first-grade primer. Pearl would do everything in her power to look like poor Cinderella and to make Carly come across as the wicked stepsister. Well, it wouldn't work. She'd pour on the sugar so thick it would turn to syrup if that's what it took. She had to stay one step ahead of the witch to make sure she didn't have an opportunity to get Cooper alone. Not that he couldn't take care of himself, but that conniving woman would use any and every opportunity to take advantage of his sweet but naïve nature.

Pearl cocked her head slightly and laid her head on Carly's shoulder. "Well, aren't you sweet? That's very neighborly of you, and I wish I could take you up on it. But I'll be busy all day getting the old farmhouse livable and won't take time to join you for lunch. However, after a hard day's work, it will be nice to clean up and join you for supper."

"Good. We'll look forward to it, won't we dear?" When Cooper didn't respond, Carly punched him. "Dear, I said we'll look forward to Pearl having supper with us tomorrow night."

He blotted his lip with his napkin and nodded. "Uh . . . of course."

Pearl's eyes lit up as she gazed across the table. "Thank you, Coop. Then I shall make a point to be here, but I'm warning you both, I'll probably look a fright after working all day."

Carly feigned a smile. "Oh, don't you worry about how you look. We won't even notice, will we sweetheart?"

Cooper shook his head. "Of course not."

Pearl pushed her plate aside and placed her elbows on the table with her chin resting on her clasped hands. With her gaze focused on Coop, she smiled as if she'd just won a prize. "Then, I'll make a point to be here, although I'll be so exhausted that I'll probably be poor company. The house is in worse shape than I had imagined. It's time like these that I realize how much it means to have a man around to help take care of things. Carly, I hope you realize how blessed you are. I can knock down spider webs and mop floors. But the roof leaks and the screens all need replacing. I simply don't know how I'll manage to get the place livable again, without a man around to help. It's times like these that I feel so alone."

"I can certainly sympathize with you, you poor dear. After all, I've been a widow, myself, but of course, you remember that don't you?" Carly swallowed hard. If her remark came across with the animosity with which it was peppered, so be it. If Pearl Greene thought she was being subtle, she needed more practice. It was plain to see she was attempting to arouse Coop's sympathy so he'd volunteer to spend time with her at the farmhouse. Well, it wasn't about to happen.

Emma walked into the room with her nightgown on, complaining she was sleepy. Carly said, "Did you brush your teeth?"

"Yes'm."

"Then, why don't you ask your Aunt Pearl to tuck you in bed. I'm sure she'd love the opportunity. Would you mind, Pearl?"

"Mind? Of course, not." But the way she stomped away with the child in tow, one would've thought she very much minded.

Pearl exited Emma's room and left in a huff.

Later that night, Cooper lay in bed trying to sort out the earlier conversation between Carly and Pearl. There was something strange taking place, though he couldn't discern what or why. Carly was being so congenial it was not only baffling, it was downright scary. "Honey, I thought—" He shrugged. "Never mind."

"Please finish." She snuggled closer, with her head resting on his shoulder. "What is it you thought?"

"I thought . . . I thought the chicken was delicious."

She smiled. "Thank you. Goodnight, sweetheart."

"Carly, is there something you'd like to talk about?"

"Now? I don't think so. What might you be referring to?"

"I thought you were—"

She snickered. "What are you trying to say, Coop?"

"Well, I thought you were very sweet to Pearl."

"Thank you, darling. You convinced me that I have no reason to be otherwise. You haven't changed your mind, have you?"

"I don't suppose so." He rolled toward her and kissed her

forehead. "Have I told you lately how much I love you?"

"Yes, but I'll sleep better tonight if you'll remind me again."

CHAPTER 6

Cooper was pleasantly surprised to see the work crew already there when he arrived at the new house. Perhaps his pep talk last week about getting started on time sunk in. But as he drew nearer, it became apparent the three on the roof weren't working, but were staring in the same direction.

Cooper said, "What have you fellows found so intriguing that it's preventing you from working?"

Burt grabbed a hammer and stammered. "Nothing boss."

Unconvinced, Coop crawled up on the ladder and looked out. Feeling his face grow hot, he yelled, "I ought to fire all three of you. Get off the roof. Now!"

"Aww, boss, we ain't done no harm. She goes to bathe every morning about this time."

"Then, I'll give you something else to do every morning and you can work on the roof in the heat of the day."

As they climbed down the ladder, Andy said, "I wonder who

she is?"

Burt's lip curled. "I don't know her name, but she's a looker. However, it's obvious she ain't got nothing but her looks. She came by my house one night about dark, wanting something to eat. The wife gave her a couple slices of light bread and a glass of buttermilk and told her not to come back begging."

Cooper said, "Solly, do you know the girl?"

"Me? No, and if my wife hears about this, I'm ruined. I'd be grateful if we drop the subject. It ain't no secret how jealous Rhoda is. If I so much as talk to another woman, she makes my life miserable. If she hears we were on the roof, sneaking a peek, she'll divorce me for sure."

Burt cackled. "A peek? Is that what you call it? You were the first one here this morning, Solly."

"Aww, Burt, that ain't so and you know it. I barely looked. Honest, Mr. Flanigan, I was up here to work and for no other reason."

"Stop worrying, Solly. No one's gonna tell Rhoda, unless it happens again and if it does, I'll personally approach all the wives."

Andy's jaw dropped. "You'd do that, Mr. Flanigan?"

"Without a minute's hesitation." He turned his back to them and walked away, hiding his smile. The shock on their faces was proof enough he'd have no more problems with them.

At 11:30, he called for the fellows to break for lunch. As he started across the field on his way home, Pearl seemed to dart out from nowhere.

"Hi Coop. I just finished mopping and had to wait outside for the floors to dry, so I was hoping I could come over and talk with you."

"Fine. Carly will have dinner ready. Come eat with us."

She twisted a lock of hair around her finger. "I'm too distraught to eat a thing, but I have to talk to someone and there's no one else I can confide in. I've always been able to count on you to listen to me."

He had no desire to stand there and chat, yet he was such a softy when it came to a female in distress—even when it was Pearl Greene. Seeing the moisture welling in her eyes and hearing the tremor in her voice, it would seem cruel to walk away.

" Coop, I've been so lonely, and I think you know it didn't just begin after Ed died. I've been lonesome for a very long time. I know Ed loved me in his own way, but I needed more. I never realized how much I missed you until I sat across the table from you last night. My heart was so heavy, I could hardy swallow my food."

"Pearl, I don't know where you're going with this conversation, and I'm truly sorry that you're lonely but I'm a married man."

She thrust her hand over her heart as if she were shocked. Sobbing, she said, "Is that what you think of me? I'm quite aware of your love for your wife and I'd never do nothing to jeopardize your happiness. Just because I said I've missed you, you assume I want to have an illicit rendezvous with a married man? I can't decide if you think that highly of yourself, or that lowly of me."

He cleared his throat. "Then I'm sorry if I jumped to an erroneous conclusion." He reached in his back pocket, pulled out a handkerchief and handed to her. "Stop crying, Pearl. If I hurt your feelings, I apologize."

She wiped her tears and whimpered, "Forget it. I was stupid for thinking I had at least one close friend with whom I could confide." With trembling lips, she said, "I should've died instead of Ed. He could've survived without me. I longed to feel his arms around me and to hear him say he loved me. But Ed's way of showing love was to reach in the cash register and hand me cash. I wish someone would tell me what I've done to turn everyone against me. Even my boys never come around, anymore." She buried her face in her hands and sobbed. "I wish I were dead."

"You don't mean that, Pearl."

"I mean every word of it. Tell me, Coop, what reason do I have for living? No one cares. Not even the one I thought to be my best friend . . . the one I foolishly thought would be there for me, come what may."

Obsessed with guilt, Cooper stepped forward and wrapped his arms around her. "Please, Pearl. I'm sorry for sounding so callous, but I thought you were saying . . . well, I suppose you know what I thought. Forgive me?"

He looked up on the roof when he heard a cat whistle and saw his work crew taking their lunch break and staring in his direction. He knew what they thought, but they were wrong. There was no denying that Pearl was a good-looking female, but regardless of what they might think, he had eyes for only one woman, and it wasn't Pearl Greene. Mumbling, he said, "I've got to get home for lunch, Pearl. I hope you'll take Carly up on her offer and have supper with us this evening."

"Thanks, but I'm sure Carly wants you all to herself whenever you get home at night, and I don't blame her. I'd feel the same way if you were my husband. Besides, she'd be bored listening to us talking about such mundane things. Ed always took care of business, and I have no idea what to do. I brought a couple of ham sandwiches. I thought we could go for a ride while you're on your break and park somewhere, where we won't have so many eyes focused in our direction. Those men make me nervous. Did you see how they were all staring while you were hugging me?"

He gave a shrug as if it didn't matter, but it did matter. It mattered a lot. He felt like a heel. Not because he'd done anything wrong, but because of how it could be perceived. Though they'd never confront him, they'd have cause to consider him a hypocrite. After all, he'd condemned them for looking at a woman, while it appeared he was meeting one on the sly. He recalled his pastor preaching a sermon on avoiding all appearances of evil. Why didn't he walk away the minute Pearl walked up?

"Cooper, why don't we drive over to my place? I'll get the ledger and we can sit under the big oak tree, eat our sandwiches and go over the store figures."

"Sorry, Pearl, but I need to get home. Carly is expecting me for lunch. You and I can go over your affairs after supper, tonight."

She snickered.

"What's funny?"

"I was just thinking about what you said about going over my affairs. I've never had an affair, except with you." She bit her lip and winked. "Have you, Coop? Had an affair with anyone other than me?"

He could feel a flush rising to his cheeks. It was true he came close to marrying Pearl at one time. But an affair? It wasn't an affair. Not even close. It was a lack of judgment and nothing else. She knew it. Why was she wanting to make something out of something that never happened?

"I made you blush. So there was someone other than me. Well, I'm not surprised. You're a very handsome man, Coop. I'm sure it's been difficult keeping the women away."

He fought the urge to argue there was no affair, but not wanting to be reminded of a low point in his life, he chose to drop the subject. "Carly and I will be expecting you for supper. Goodbye, Pearl."

"Are you sure that's a good idea? I need you, Coop—your advice, I mean. But I think Carly may be a bit jealous of me. I'm afraid your wife doesn't really want me around."

"That's ridiculous. She has no reason to be jealous. Besides, it was her idea to invite you over. It's what she wants."

"But is it what you want?"

Pretending not to hear, he said, "I'll see you tonight, The fellows should be finished with their lunch. I'm afraid they're more interested in what's going on over here than what I've hired them to do. I need to go, Pearl."

She snickered. "I suppose we fooled them, since there is nothing going on over here. Is there, Cooper?"

His brows formed a vee. "No. No, there isn't." He walked away, wondering if he should tell Carly of the surprise meeting or if it would be better not to mention it. He'd been shocked at her change in attitude toward Pearl. Had he finally convinced her that he had no feelings for the woman, or was Carly simply putting on an act? But why would she do that? He'd feel much better if she'd stop encouraging Pearl to spend time with them. Even if Carly were making an effort to overcome her animosity toward Pearl, he didn't know how much longer she could keep it up if Pearl continued to openly and unabashedly make a play for him. The woman was definitely coming on to him. Wasn't she? Or was he simply flattering himself by imagining her actions were more romantic than platonic?

Pearl had taken so much of his time, he debated whether he should forget about lunch or go on home and grab a bite to eat. Carly would be waiting. He watched Pearl drive off, then walked over and gave instructions to the work crew, letting them know what he'd expect after he returned home from lunch.

Carly was sitting in the swing on the porch when he arrived.

"Why are you so late? I fried fish but it's cold, already. I'm sorry. I tried to keep it warm, but now it's soggy. What happened?"

"What do you mean, what happened? Nothing happened, Carly. I can't always go by a clock. I resent being quizzed when I've done nothing to warrant it."

Her brow creased. "Quizzed? Good heavens, sweetheart. Is that what you thought I was doing? I was merely attempting an apology for your lunch being cold. You look beat. I assumed something happened at the site that required you to stay later than usual. Would you like to talk about it?"

He should go ahead and tell her that Pearl came to the work site and detained him. There was no reason not to tell her. It wasn't as if he had anything to do with her showing up at lunchtime. "Honey, I'm sorry. I was ready to come home at 11:30. I'd already told the fellows to break for lunch."

"Coop, I realize things come up that are beyond your control. If I sounded cross, I'm sorry. I really didn't mean for it to come across that way. The fish would've been better if I hadn't covered them while they were hot. It's my fault they aren't as crispy, but I made a blueberry cobbler, so that should make up for it. Come on in the kitchen and get washed up while I fix you a plate. I'm sure you're eager to get back to work."

He sucked in a long breath of air and let it out slowly. She was right. He was eager to get back and he had no time to go into a lengthy explanation. If he mentioned Pearl's name, Carly would spend thirty minutes grilling him. "Where's Emma?"

"She's taking a nap. She wanted to wait for you to come home, but she got up so early this morning, she could hardly hold her eyes open long enough to eat her lunch."

Cooper finished his fish and potatoes, then pushed back from the table. "Gotta get back, hon. Thanks for lunch."

"But you haven't had dessert."

"Save it for tonight. I really need to run. I was hoping to have the roof finished today, but it doesn't look like it's gonna happen."

"I understand. I'm sorry you're running behind time. I know how you like to stay on schedule. Do you think you'll be late for supper?"

"No, I'll be here on time. Pearl's coming."

"Pearl?"

"Uh . . . yes. Don't you remember you invited her?"

"Of course. But it sounded as if you might be saying . . . forget it. You need to scoot." She stood on her tippy toes for a kiss. "Goodbye, sweetheart. I hope the remainder of your day goes much better than the first half."

He placed his palms on either side of her face and kissed her. "So do I, dear. So do I."

CHAPTER 7

Carly sat quietly at the table after supper as Pearl Greene pulled out a ledger and slid her chair close to Cooper's.

She said, "Carly, I'm sure this bores you. Please don't feel the need to sit here and listen to this. I know I should've learned more about our business dealings before Ed died, but I Suwannee, this is all so frustrating. If it weren't for Coop willing to help me figure this all out, I declare, I don't know what I'd do."

Carly bit the inside of her cheek. Did she dare leave? Not that she didn't trust her husband, but she hated the thought of giving Pearl the satisfaction of having him all alone. But what if Pearl's motive was to make her look like the jealous wife while appearing to be the sweet, innocent victim? Swallowing hard, she slid her chair back. "Thank you, Pearl. It must be extremely difficult for you to understand figures posted in a ledger. I'm sure my husband can help you decipher them. So if you two will excuse me, I think I'll take Emma for a walk."

Coop's eyes widened. "But . . . but it's dark outside, honey."

"Not too dark at all. The moon is full and Emma will love it. It'll be fun." She bent down and pecked him on the forehead. "We won't be gone long." Carly pulled three cookies from the cookie jar, wrapped them in a napkin and stuck them in her apron pocket. Just as she suspected, Emma was delighted at the thought of taking a stroll in the moonlight.

Emma chattered nonstop as she skipped beside Carly. "This is fun, Mama. Can we do this every night?"

"If we did it every night, it would cease to be special. But we'll do it again one day."

"Can we please walk down to the river?"

"That's a great idea. The moon will be beautiful shining on the water."

Carly felt guilty that she hadn't thought to take Emma on a moonlight walk before and silently vowed to do it more often— next time with Coop. She reached in her pocket and pulled out the napkin holding the three oatmeal cookies.

"Cookies?" The glee in Emma's voice made Carly almost forget her husband was at home alone with that conniving woman. "I brought one for me and two for you. We'll sit on the bank, eat our treat and watch the fish jump."

"And maybe we'll see the Swamp Angel?"

Carly sighed. "Sweetheart, she's not an angel and no one lives in the swamp. I like that you have a vivid imagination, but sometimes you tell things you've dreamed up as if it's truth, and when that happens, it becomes a lie. We can pretend a Swamp Angel lives here, but we must say, "What if . . ."

"I don't understand."

When you make up a story, say "What if a girl lived in the swamp and we found out she was an angel. By saying 'what if,' it indicates it hasn't really happened, but it's something we can pretend."

"But I know she's real."

"I didn't say the girl isn't real. I know she exists, but I also know that she's no angel and she has a home somewhere. Maybe her family moved into that little shanty over on Callahan road."

"Is it okay if I pretend she's a swamp angel?"

"Of course! As I said, I love it that you have an imagination. You might think about writing down some of the stories you make up."

"Like a real writer?"

"Why not? You could write fiction and satisfy that yearning of yours in a positive way."

Emma grinned. "Then I know what I'll be when I'm grown up. I'll be a writer. But didn't you tell me fiction means it's not true? What if I write about something really happens, like seeing a swamp angel? Then it's called a true story, right?"

Carly was glad they'd reached the river and she could change the subject before she'd wind up irritated that she was not getting through to Emma. The moon shimmering on the calm waters couldn't have been more beautiful. She reached in her pocket and handed the wrapped cookies to Emma, then pulled off her apron and spread it on the grass. "This looks like a good spot to sit and eat our cookies." She heard a splash, and Emma squealed with delight. Carly smiled. "Oh, I missed it. Did you see the fish jump?"

Emma ran down the bank toward the water. "It was no fish, Mama. It's the swamp angel."

Carly hurried down the bank and grabbed her daughter by the hand. "Emma Flanigan I'm gonna take a switch to you if you insist on telling . . ." She stopped and thrust her hand over her mouth. "Oh, m'goodness."

The girl yelled, "Sorry, ma'am. I had to stop bathing in the daylight. I didn't expect nobody to come around at night. I'd leave but my clothes are hanging on a bush."

Emma said, "I'll take them to you."

Carly said, "Emma, I don't want you getting too close to the water. Why don't you and I turn our heads while she gets out and gets into her clothes?"

The water splashed, bushes rustled and a few minutes later the girl called out. "I'm dressed, and I'll be leaving now. Didn't mean to cause no trouble."

Carly told Emma she could open her eyes, then yelled, "No harm done." She motioned for the girl to join them. "I understand you saved our little girl."

The girl appeared skittish as if she didn't know whether to stay or run. Then slowly walking toward Carly and Emma, she nodded slightly. "I reckon it's the only good thing I've ever done, so I won't ever forget how good it felt to know I didn't let her drown."

Emma stretched the apron as far as it would go, then plopped down. "Sit down with us. Mama brought us all a cookie. Didn't you Mama? She brought three. One for her, one for me and one for you."

The girl gazed at the napkin in Emma's hands. "Did you say a cookie?"

Carly observed the longing on the young girl's face, as if she hadn't eaten all day. "Actually, Emma, I'm not very hungry. I had a big supper. Maybe your friend would like my cookie, too."

The light in Emma's eyes made the full moon look dull in comparison. "You called her my friend, Mama. I told you she was a real swamp angel. Now do you believe me?"

"Honey, I knew she was real, but I'll let her explain to you that she's not a swamp angel." Carly handed a cookie to Emma and two to the girl. "What's your name and where do you live?"

The girl took a bite of cookie and licked her lips. "This is good, ma'am. Real good. My name is Eliza Clementine Graham. . . but you can call me . . . uh, Clementine?"

"What a beautiful name. Did you know there's a song written about you?"

"About me, ma'am?"

Carly chuckled. "It's a ballad about a girl with your same name. I don't know all the words, but it's rather sad. It says something about, "You are lost and gone forever, oh, my darling, Clementine."

"Yes'm, I reckon you might say that could rightly be about me."

Eager to understand the sadness behind those beautiful eyes, Carly reluctantly held onto her thoughts.

Emma said, "And she's a swamp angel, so she lives in the swamp. Right, 'Lemon Time?'"

"Yes, and no. I ain't proud to have to admit that I've done my share of sinning. It's true I've been living in the swamp, but your mama's right. I ain't no angel. Far from it. I set up camp here, thinking these swamps didn't b'long to nobody. But if you'll let me stay the night, ma'am, I promise to move on first thing tomorrow."

Carly's brow furrowed. "How old are you, child, and where is your family. I'm sure they're very worried about you."

"I'm sixteen, ma'am, but ain't nobody worried about me."

"I find that hard to believe."

"It's true. I was a foundling when I was shuttled from one foster home to another, but I reckon I was a handful and nobody wanted me. I kept running away and was finally put in an orphanage. It was the best thing that ever happened to me. Then, a while ago, I ran away again. I won't never be going back and I don't 'spect nobody cares."

"Do you mind if I asked why you ran away?

She hung her head. "I'd rather not say, if you don't mind. It might not be fit for the young'un's ears."

Carly's imagination soared, though she tried to hide her shock.

"Well, it's really none of my business, but I'm thankful you were at the river, else our little Emma wouldn't be here. Why don't you go spend the night at our house tonight and tomorrow we'll come up with a solution to your dilemma. Surely, you understand that you can't continue living in the swamp."

"That's mighty swell of you to want to help me, lady, but I ain't got no money. I'm dreadfully sorry about squattin' on your property. I promise to leave at first light in the morning."

"Well, we need to be getting back to the house. My husband will begin to worry." Carly held out her hand. "Please come with us, Clementine, and I'll feed you what we had left over from supper."

The girl appeared unmoved until she heard Carly mention food. "Yes'm, I reckon I could go with you, just for the night."

Emma watched the girl reach for a knapsack stuck in a low tree branch. "Whatcha got in that bag?"

Carly reprimanded her daughter. "Sweetheart, that's very rude. It's none of our business."

The girl smiled. "I don't mind." Then spreading the top of the bag open, she said, "Take a look." She pulled out a tin cup, plate, a small pot, a fork, a hunting knife, a large box of matches and a small coin purse.

"What's in that little paper bag?"

"A hook and line." Before Emma had a chance to ask the next question, the girl said, "I love to fish. I like to eat them, too. What about you?"

Emma was more concerned with the bulky content still inside the bag. "What's that thing at the bottom?"

Carly apologized once more for her daughter's curiosity, but the girl shrugged it off, then answered, "It's a dress and my army blanket. I didn't pull it out because it's folded nice and tight."

"You were in the army?"

"No, but a very dear friend was, and he gave me the blanket."

Emma looked around. "Where is he?"

Carly was suddenly interested in hearing an answer that might provide a clue to the girl's plight..

"A long way off. I probably won't never see him again."

"Oh."

For once, Carly was wishing the little busybody would press further, but her inquisitive mind jumped to another subject.

"Where's your bed?"

"I don't need a bed. I lay the blanket on the ground, and I'm quite comfortable."

"Is that all you have?"

Carly rolled her eyes. "Emma, that's enough."

"It's okay, ma'am. She reminds me of myself at that age. I've always been accused of asking too many questions, but I think it's good to be curious. It indicates a thirst for knowledge.. The contents of this bag is all I have, Emma, but it's also all I need."

Satisfied with the answers, Emma grabbed the girl's hand on the walk home. "I like you. You're my best friend, Lemon Time."

A smile crossed her lips. "I like you, too, Emma, and I'm glad we're friends. Suppose you call me Clemmie. It's much easier to say."

Seeing her smile for the first time, Carly was encouraged. If anyone could break through that defensive, independent shell, Emma would be the one to do it.

CHAPTER 8

After an hour of getting very little done, Cooper closed the ledger, aware that Pearl was more interested in rehashing old times than working on the books. When he suggested it was a lovely moonlit night and they should wait for Carly and Emma outside on the porch, he was surprised when Pearl agreed whole-heartedly. She rushed out to the swing, slid over and patted the seat next to her.

He shook his head. "Thanks, but I'm too nervous to sit."

"I didn't realize I still had that effect on you."

"I beg your pardon?"

"Coop, remember the night we sat together in the swing over at Aunt Pat's when Uncle Robert died? It was a night much like this one. Full moon, cool breeze. Of course, we were much younger. But that's all water under the bridge. Right?"

Suspecting that he was expected to remember her Aunt Pat and Uncle Robert, he simply made an incoherent mumble.

"Oh m'goodness, you don't remember, do you? It was the

night we first met. I remember it as if it were yesterday. You came to the Wake with your sister. You were wearing a blue shirt and dungarees. You looked across the room at me and when you winked, I Suwannee, my heart did somersaults. We sneaked outside and sat in the swing together."

"We did?" His eyes squinted as the vague memory came back, but he and Pearl were apparently remembering the night differently. His sister had pleaded with him to go with her, though he insisted he didn't know her friend Pearl, nor the deceased uncle. The thought of staying all night, shut up in the house with a horde of boisterous strangers who pretended to be there to offer condolences, made him question such a strange tradition. Yet, he always found it difficult to say no to his only sister. It was even worse than he had imagined.

Wanting to get out of the smoke-filled house, he went outside, and found there were almost as many people on the porch as in the house. He sat in the only seat available. He now vaguely remembered a pretty young girl walking out and asking if he minded if she sat beside him. She introduced herself as Pearl Watson from Coffee Springs and a few weeks later, he saw her in the hall at school and discovered she had moved to Marl to live with her Aunt Pat.

Pearl smiled. "You do remember, don't you?"

Cooper wanted to deny it, sensing she would be eager to help him recall every detail. He was still stalking back and forth on the porch when Carly and the girls approached the house.

He hurried down the steps to meet her. "What happened? I was getting worried." His brow lifted, silently questioning why the girl who rescued Emma was with them.

Carly grinned, knowing Pearl chose the swing in hopes that Cooper would choose to sit with her. However, he was much smarter than that. "I'm sorry if we worried you, honey. I didn't intend to be gone so long." With her hand on the girl's shoulder, she said, "Coop, darling, I don't think I have to introduce you to Eliza Clementine Graham, since you two have already met."

He tipped his head, "The name's Cooper. My wife and I owe you a debt of gratitude, Miss.."

The girl curtsied slightly. "Nice to make your acquaintance, Mr. Cooper, but y'all ain't beholding to me. Just reckon I done what anybody woulda done in my place."

If Pearl's brow had shot up any higher, it would've reached her widow's peak.

Carly smiled, then placing her hand on the girl's shoulder, said, "Clementine dear, allow me to introduce you to our good friend, Pearl Greene."

Clemmie extended her hand, but dropped it to her side when Pearl made no effort to respond to the gesture. "Nice to make your acquaintance, ma'am."

Pearl allowed her gaze to travel from the top of the girl's head, to her feet, before muttering, "Likewise, I'm sure."

Carly chirped, "I'm glad to see you and Coop had time to finish going over the ledger. It must be a relief to know that it's over."

Pearl made an effort to interject, though Carly pretended not to notice. "Honey, I've invited Clementine to stay with us tonight. She hasn't eaten, so if you and Pearl will excuse me, I need to go inside and fix her a plate." Emma was pulling the girl by the hand. "Come see my room, Clemmie. You can sleep with me tonight if you want to."

After the girls left, Pearl said, "Carly, hold on." With Carly holding the door partially open, Pearl looked at Cooper. "Don't you have anything to say, because if you don't, I'm not sure I can hold my tongue much longer, and I'm confident you're even more concerned about this situation than I am."

Carly smiled. "Oh, m'goodness, Pearl, you're shaking like a leaf. Whatever has you so agitated?"

"Agitated? I never said I was agitated. Just concerned. But really, Carly, are you sure you know what you're doing? I've heard countless horror stories of people who meant well and wound up getting stabbed in their sleep. If you start feeding her it'll be like throwing a bone to a mangy old dog that shows up at your back door—you'll never get rid of her. I'm sure Coop will agree with me that you never should've brought her here. She didn't need to know where you live. The sooner you get rid of her, the better. I don't mean to criticize, but frankly I don't know what you were thinking."

Carly shot a glance at her husband expecting him to speak out and commend her for her Christian efforts. Instead, he quickly lowered his head without commenting, She slung her long hair over her left shoulder, and blurted, "I'm sorry you don't approve, Pearl, but the verse, 'I was hungry, and you fed me,' weighed heavily on my mind, the moment I found her, all alone in the swamp. Jesus said, 'When you have done it unto one of the least of these, my brethren, you have done it unto me." She cocked her head. "Tell me, Pearl, would you have done less?"

"If she has nowhere to go, then you can bet your bottom dollar she brought it on herself. Mark my word, Carly, you're inviting trouble. Emma seemed to have the idea the girl is staying overnight, but I'm sure Coop won't allow that to happen."

It was none of Pearl Greene's business if she and Coop took a dozen homeless waifs into their home. Carly's blood boiled when her husband sat there as if he were mute. Why was he not putting Pearl in her place?

Pearl appeared to interpret his silence as a green light to continue her fiery diatribe. "Why, a woman came into the feed store one day and told us about her sister, Ruby, who took in a homeless stranger, considering it her Christian duty to give her a place to stay until she could find a job. Are you interested in knowing how that turned out?"

"Not particularly."

"Well, I think you should know. If you aren't concerned about your own welfare, you should consider Coop and little Emma."

Carly was sick and tired of hearing Pearl refer to Cooper as Coop. She considered that her very own affectionate name for her husband. He was known as Cooper to everyone else. She swallowed hard. Why was she concentrating on things that didn't really matter? Had she become so bitter that if Pearl Greene said the sky was blue, she'd argue it was red? Though her thoughts wandered, it didn't appear she'd missed much.

Pearl was still ranting. "After a month of sponging off Ruby and her husband, Ruby tried to throw her out. But lo and behold the woman refused to leave and would you believe she ended up stealing Ruby's husband? It's a fact. Poor Ruby had no alternative but to move in with her sister, after her husband and the girl booted her out."

"Thank you, Pearl, but Clementine isn't here to steal my husband, although I understand why you might be concerned. We didn't mean to keep you so late. I should get in the kitchen and get the poor child something to eat. " She reached out her hand. "Goodnight, dear. Please, do drop in again sometime."

"Child, my foot. She's about as full grown as she'll ever get."

Carly smiled, turned and walked away, leaving Pearl with her mouth gaping open. "Well, Coop, I do believe your wife just said that I've overstayed my welcome."

"I'm sure she didn't mean for it to sound so blunt. He crooked his arm. "Allow me to help you down the porch steps. I've been intending to put up a rail." Wrapping her arm in his, she smiled. "Well, aren't you sweet to offer to escort me home."

She was doing it again. How could that woman take whatever he said and twist it to fit her narrative, leaving him wondering how he got himself into such a mess.

"The moon is bright, Pearl. You should be able to see the way home without my help."

With a coy smile, she murmured, "I understand your hesitancy. Coop, I want you to know what a relief it is to know you're here for me. I don't have to tell you that you're the reason I felt I needed to come back to Cartersville. I had no one else to turn to. You've been great to give me advice when I needed it. Now, if you would allow me to give you a little advice . . ."

"I wasn't aware I needed any. What's on your mind, Pearl?"

"It's obvious that Carly's compassion is getting in the way of common sense. If I were you, I'd think twice before letting that little swamp urchin take up residence, here. Anyone can look at her and tell she's up to no good."

"Really, Pearl? And how did you come to such a conclusion?"

"Coop, I wouldn't expect you to see the signs, but trust me a woman can tell. She's young and beautiful and is probably accustomed to getting any man she sets her sites on." She reached up and straightened his collar. With the corner of her lip slightly lifted, she said, "To be honest, if you weren't a married man, I might even be tempted, too. It wouldn't surprise me at all if that girl decided the day she handed Emma to you that she liked what she saw."

He ran his hand over the back of his neck. "I know you mean well, Pearl, but—"

Pearl reached for his hand. "You've got to believe me—for

little Emma's sake. Get that girl out of your house, Coop. The sooner the better. I wouldn't even wait until morning. I don't know what Carly was thinking, bringing the little wench here."

"Goodnight, Pearl."

Cooper lumbered into the kitchen just as Carly sat a plate piled with food in front of the girl. Who was she? Where did she come from? Were her parents searching for her or was she truly all alone? He couldn't imagine what gave Pearl the idea the innocent-looking creature was no good. All he saw was a sweet-looking, very hungry teenager, who saved Emma's life. Even so, he couldn't dismiss the nagging thought that Pearl's warning shouldn't be so easily dismissed.

Smiling at Emma, who had pulled her chair so close to the young girl's that she barely had elbow room, he walked over and slid his daughter's chair back in place. Though Emma's lip formed a pout, she said nothing. It was evident his little girl was smitten. He could only hope Carly knew what she was doing by taking in a stranger they knew absolutely nothing about. If she'd been kicked out of her home, her parents might've had just reason.

Emma hadn't taken her eyes off her new friend. "Clemmie, when you finish eating, we can go play in my room."

Cooper spoke up. "It isn't her bedtime, sugar, but it is yours, so give us a hug and run jump in bed."

Emma didn't put up an argument but ran over and hugged her new friend. "See you in the morning."

After Emma left, Clementine said, "The food was delicious, ma'am but I don't want to put you folks out no longer, so I reckon I'll be on my way."

Attempting to hide his apprehension of harboring a runaway, Cooper jumped on the opportunity. "Well, you know where we live, so if you decide to move into the area, we hope you'll feel free to come back to visit." When his wife's glare seemed to cast daggers his way, he knew he'd said the wrong thing.

"What my husband means is that you are welcome to stay here as long as need be, but when the time comes that you must move on, please don't forget us. I think you'll be comfortable on the back porch. Cooper screened it in and I moved a cot out there shortly after we moved here."

Recalling the reason she placed the cot on the back porch three years ago brought a lump to Carly's throat. She had moved it from the back room in order to make room for the baby's crib. Swallowing her pain, she feigned a smile and gave Cooper instructions to bring a pillow and the heavy Sunbonnet Sue quilt, as the weather was a bit cooler on the porch.

CHAPTER 9

It was a lovely night. A slight breeze blew from the North, the sky was glistening with stars, and the sound of crickets and frogs had a comforting melodic sound.

Cooper walked back out to the screened-in porch with the quilt, sheets and a pillow. "Clementine, is it?"

"Yessir."

"That's a mighty pretty name. I'm sure you're tired, so my wife and I will bid you a good night." He wrapped his arm around Carly's waist. "Shall we go, dear? I'm sure she's eager to get to sleep." Seeing Carly recoil at his words, he'd thought it worth a try. It seemed to irritate her that he would even suggest she would go to bed before knowing all there was to know about the girl.

Cooper winced. This was exactly the way it began with the abused mongrel she rescued from the swamp. For weeks, she acted as if she'd been appointed as the dog's guardian angel and it was her duty to keep a constant eye on him. After nursing him back to health and becoming attached to the animal, old man Grover Abrams, a woodcutter from a nearby county, showed up claiming to be the owner. Carly was heartbroken, certain the dog would be subjected to more abuse.

Now, she'd attached herself to a two-legged stray, which scared the daylights out of him. He wasn't sure if he was more frightened at the possibility that someone would come to claim the girl, or at the thought that no one might.

Carly grabbed the linens from his arms and spat out an emphatic "Thank you, Cooper!" However, the way her jaw jutted forward when she spoke, he was confident the three razor-sharp words could've easily shaved off Prince Albert's beard in one whack.

His first reaction was to strike back. He caught his bottom lip through his teeth long enough to prevent him from lashing out and further exasperating a tense situation.

It wasn't that he was angry at Carly for wanting to help the down and out—he'd always loved that about her—but not at this vulnerable time in her life. For all they knew, the girl could be running from the law. Hadn't Carly gone through enough heartache? Hadn't he? Not wanting to stir the pot further, he lifted a shoulder in a slight shrug. "I'll bid you ladies a good night. I'm bushed." Disappointed that his wife showed no interest in going with him, he turned and headed to bed.

Carly lingered after her husband left and would like to have stayed longer to learn more about their mysterious guest, but she knew the girl was tired and it would be selfish to keep her up longer. On the way to her bedroom Carly paused in front of the nursery. Pressing her lips together, she eased open the door, walked over and sat in the Boston rocker. Rocking back and forth, humming a lullaby, she imagined what it would've been like to have held a baby in her arms. It could've been ten minutes or thirty, she had no idea how long she sat there before walking over to the crib and propping the little teddy bear upright in the corner of the bed. For a split second, she thought she could see a sleeping baby, snuggled under the pastel blanket that she spent weeks crocheting. The image disappeared when she blinked. She swallowed hard, wishing it could've lingered a few seconds longer.

Whether the words were in her thoughts or if she said them aloud, she couldn't be sure. But the message was as distinct as if it were written in bold letters on the wall. *It's time.* And with the words, came a clear understanding. For too long, Carly had floundered through each day, always looking backward, reliving the horrible moment when she felt the rickety old ladder moving from beneath her feet, landing her on the floor. The agonizing guilt, which had caused her to struggle to get out of bed every morning had escalated to the point she often felt as if she were losing her sanity. Not only had she made herself miserable over something she couldn't change, but her negative attitude was affecting her relationship with her husband. She murmured, "I agree. It *is* time, Lord, but I can't do it, alone. Please, help me!" A peace she hadn't felt in a long time came over her, when a verse she learned as a child, came to mind. *"Call upon me and I will answer . . . "* Why had she waited so long?

Her heart hammered at the thought of finally moving in a forward direction. She knew exactly what she needed to do and she couldn't let Cooper or anyone else talk her out of it. Why had she waited so long to agree with God?"

After leaving the nursery, she quietly tiptoed into their bedroom and slid next to her sleeping husband. Though it was late, there were too many questions whizzing around in her head to even think of sleeping. What would Coop say if she told him she planned to encourage Clementine to move in with them? Perhaps he'd question her judgment in the beginning, but knowing the poor girl was at the mercy of the world, wouldn't he agree it would be the Christian thing to do?

CHAPTER 10

Garth Graham and his wife Gracie sat in the Sheriff's office, waiting for the sheriff to get in. The secretary had made a fresh pot of coffee on the little electric hot plate and assured them that Hobie would be in shortly. After the secretary went back into her office, Gracie whispered, "Honey, are you sure we're doing the right thing?"

"For crying out loud, Gigi, we've gone over this a dozen times. You want to find her, don't you?"

"Of course I do, but you know how folks around here love to gossip. I'm not sure we need to display our dirty laundry in front of the whole town, and that's exactly what we'll be doing if we tell Hobie why she left. You know what they'll say."

Garth blew out a long puff of air. Then in a display of compassion—whether real or contrived—he took her hand in his and gazed into her eyes. "Is that what worries you? You're concerned about what people might say?"

The sheriff walked in, hung his hat on a wall rack and held out his hand. "Good to see you, both. It's been a while. Pauline called to tell me you were here. Sorry, it took me so long, but I had business to attend to in Hacoda. I see my girl, Friday, made you coffee. I'm glad. She's an angel." He pulled off his coat and hung it across the back of his chair. "It's a bit nippy outside, but I love it. I'm originally from North Carolina and it's taken me a while to get accustomed to the hot, humid South Alabama summers. I've probably told you before that I met my sweetie when I was stationed at Fort Rucker."

Garth nodded.

"Well, being that all her family lived in these parts, I knew she'd never be happy if I took her away, and since I planned to go into law enforcement, I figured I could do it here, as well as I could in Charlotte." He walked around his desk, sat down and propped his feet up. "Looks like your cup's empty. I'll get Pauline to come pour you another cup. I might even drink a little myself."

Garth's patience was wearing thin, as the sheriff continued to ramble. Cutting him off, he said, "Excuse me, Hobie, but we need to state our business before Gracie loses her nerve and walks out of here. It took all I could do to get her to come with me, so if you don't mind, I'd like to say what we came to say."

"Sure, sure! I didn't realize you were in such a hurry. What's on your mind?"

Drawing a deep breath, Garth's gaze locked with his wife's. "We came to report that our daughter is missing."

The sheriff quickly jerked his feet from off the desk and leaned forward. "Oh, my lands. Missing? Little Mercy? I can't believe it." His gaze locked with Gracie's. "Don't you fret, ma'am. We'll get right on it. I promise you we'll find that sweet little thing, and we won't stop until we do."

Gracie frowned. "Thank you, but it's Ludie."

"Who?"

"Ludie."

The sheriff's shoulders drooped as he relaxed. "I understood Garth to say your daughter was missing."

"Ludie is our adopted daughter. We kept hoping to hear from her, but there's been no word. We're worried sick and we've got to find out if she's okay."

Hobie leaned back in his chair, pulled a cigar from his drawer, and held one out for Garth, who declined. "You're talking about that teenager who lives at the orphanage, aren't you?" Rubbing his hand across the back of his neck, he said, "I'll admit, you gave me a scare. I'm glad to know it's just that girl."

Gracie jumped up. "She's not 'just that girl.' She's my daughter. I think we should go, Garth. We made a mistake by coming here. Sorry to have wasted your time, Hobie. Have a good day."

The sheriff's eyes widened. "Jeepers, I didn't mean to offend you. I just meant it wasn't as serious as it would've been if Mercy was the one lost. At least the girl can find her way back to the orphanage—that is, if she really wanted to go back. Please, sit back down and let's go over the details. You say she's been gone for some time, but you're just now reporting it?"

Gracie glanced at her husband, and taking a silent cue from him, she eased back down in her chair. "I kept thinking we'd hear from her. She was always good to let us know where she was going and with whom, but I'm beginning to think something terrible has happened. I know she would've reached out before now. This just isn't like her."

Garth said, "What my wife means is that it *wasn't* like her, but Ludie pulled a few stunts before she left that seemed out of character for her." He felt Gracie's glare, but continued to focus his attention on the sheriff.

Stroking his chin, Hobie was slow to respond. "If I remember correctly, this is the same girl who ran away once before. Correct?"

Gracie picked up on the question before giving Garth an opportunity to respond. "Well, yes, but that was different."

"How so?"

"First of all, that was three years ago, and Ludie has done a lot of growing up in the past three years. She's strong-willed, for sure, but she isn't as impulsive as she was back then."

Garth nodded. "She's right, Hobie. Although Gracie likes to refer to Ludie as being strong-willed, I call it headstrong. When she makes up her mind to do something, right or wrong, nothing or no one who can change it. She's smart as a whip and has learned to think things out, unlike her impulsive behavior when she upped and ran off the first time. I can look back now and understand why she did what she did at thirteen."

"Would you mind sharing?"

Garth glanced at his wife. "I beg your pardon? I thought that was what I was doing."

"You said you could understand why she did what she did at thirteen. For me to aid in the search, I need to get into her head. If she's been gone this long, she either doesn't want to be found . . . or she's—" He rubbed his hand across his mouth. "We'll cross that bridge if we get there. Obviously, you don't know why she ran away this time, but since you say you understand why she left three years ago, I need you to start there."

"Well, it all began when I was away fighting in the war and Gracie received word that I'd been killed. Poor Gracie was trying to balance running an orphanage by herself while dealing with her grief. She hired a dirt farmer to help around the grounds, but she soon learned she needed more than what a grounds keeper could give her—and since he'd pestered her to marry him, it appeared to be a solution to a problem she couldn't fix. He paused and Gracie asked if it would be easier if she told it, but he indicated he'd finish what he started. "My sweet, trusting wife was taken advantage of by the dirty, rotten scoundrel."

"Whoa! I get that your wife had her plate full and wanted— uh, needed a man around to take care of things, but I don't understand what this has to do with the young girl running away."

"I'm getting to that. Although Gracie is very trusting, Ludie had been in enough bad orphanages before coming to Nine Gables to discern the sheep from the goats."

"I think I'm beginning to understand. The man was abusive to the girl. She didn't want to tell, so she left to get away from him."

"No."

"Then, please explain."

"She was upset that Gracie was considering marrying the goat."

Hobie picked up a pencil and appeared to write something down. Then with a sarcastic chuckle, he said "I get it. She wasn't willing to share Gracie's affection with an outsider. Typical teenage behavior. Things don't go their way, and they up and leave. I hear you."

Garth winced at the smirk on Hobie's face. "No! You aren't hearing me if that's what you thought I was saying, and Ludie is anything but the typical teenager. She has discernment that belies her years."

"Sorry, man, but I'm simply trying to draw a picture in my mind to help me understand the way the girl thinks."

Gracie cast her focus downward at her hands, which were locked together in her lap. "Perhaps I can help. Hobie, I was a total wreck three years ago, when Ludie first ran away. I was young and believed my husband to be dead. I'd only had the orphanage open for a few months when I suddenly found myself in charge of five children who needed love that I was mentally incapable of giving. A widower, a man by the name of Zeke, showed up at the door one day and asked if I'd take in his twin boys. I was awed by his devotion to his kids. He came around more than I would've liked, but I understood how much he loved the boys. Then he began doing little odd jobs around the place, before he'd leave. It made me uncomfortable since I couldn't pay him. That's when he presented me with a proposal, which seemed to make perfect sense. It would solve a huge problem for both of us."

"So you married him?"

"No. I kept putting him off. Even though Garth was reported to be dead, in my heart I still felt like a married woman. He offered to take care of the house and grounds for room and board. I needed a man around to do the things I couldn't and he needed a place to stay, so it seemed like a win-win."

"But you both were living under the same roof, am I right?"

"Well, yes . . . but he slept on a cot in the basement."

Garth gnawed his bottom lip. Why did she feel the need to explain Zeke's sleeping arrangements. It wasn't as if Hobie was questioning her reputation. Or was he?"

The sheriff's brow creased. "Mrs. Graham, I can see this is difficult for you to tell. Allow me to help you. You're a strikingly beautiful, healthy young woman. But you were lonely and a handsome widower with the same physical longings as you, showed up at a time when you were most vulnerable. He presented a solution that would meet both your needs. Your proper upbringing urged you to refuse his advances, but your fleshly desires overcame your ability to resist so you eventually allowed him to move into the orphanage."

The ridiculous scenario left Garth speechless.

The sheriff continued. "Ludie learned of your little tete-a-tete and feeling you were being hypocritical, she voiced her contempt for the man, then dealt with the situation the only way she knew how. She ran away. I think we're getting somewhere."

Garth shouted. "No! That's ludicrous. There was no tete-a-tete. Weren't you listening? She told you she felt like a married woman, and she *waited*. Waited for *me*. Even though she thought I was dead, she waited. Gracie, you were right. We should've left twenty minutes ago."

With a shoulder shrug, Hobie said, "I didn't mean to upset you, Garth. I'm simply trying to find something to go on. If I was wrong, I apologize, but it seemed to me that's what your wife was trying to say without hurting your feelings. Maybe my theory was right or maybe it was wrong, but we'll get nowhere if you're unwilling to cooperate. If Gracie says I'm on the wrong track, we'll go in a different direction. That is, if you really *want* to find the girl."

"Of course I want to find her, she's our daughter. But I can assure you that you're on the wrong track. Furthermore, I think you owe my wife an apology for those suggestive remarks."

"Fair enough. Forgive me, Gracie, if I jumped the gun, but it sounded as if you were trying to say you took the fellow into your boudoir. If that was the case, it would've made sense that a teenage girl would've considered it hypocrisy on your part. Running away when things don't go their way seems to be the way teens handle things."

"But it wasn't like that—not really."

Garth swallowed hard. *Not really?*

Gracie kept her focus on her folded hands. "I can understand how it must look to you, Hobie, but I hired Zeke to tend the gardens and make needed repairs on the house. His duties ended there."

"Fair enough. So there was never any talk of romance? He never suggested getting married so he could move his pillow upstairs?"

Tears welled in her eyes when she looked at her husband. "He wanted to . . . to marry me."

Scratching his head, Hobie said, "Whoa! Please clarify. Did you or did you not make plans to marry the fellow."

"I regret to say that I did."

Garth's teeth meshed together. "Say no more, Gracie. Our personal lives are none of his business and this has nothing to do with finding Ludie."

The sheriff said, "I know this is difficult for you, Garth, but please bear with me. We both want the same thing—to find the girl. He then went into a fictional scenario, suggesting Zeke could still be in love with Gracie. "How did Ludie feel about the upcoming marriage?"

Gracie said, "She was furious. She saw through Zeke from the beginning."

"Did she try to interfere?"

"She did. Garth was right when he said her discernment belied her years. Fortunately, I finally realized she was right about him before it was too late."

"Ah, we may be getting somewhere. If the fellow blamed Ludie for interfering in his happiness, that contempt could've festered over the years. Naturally, we're merely speculating, but you've admitted it's out of character for her not to contact you after this long. It's possible that he may have kidnapped her to seek revenge. Revenge is a terrible curse. It can dwell inside a man for years and years until it takes over his senses."

"Absurd," Garth shouted. He glanced over at his wife. "Gracie? Tell him . . . tell him that's crazy. You know that isn't what happened. He's blowing this all out of proportion."

Garth had promised Gracie before coming that he'd not mention the events leading up to Ludie's disappearance. He agreed nothing could be gained by dragging up the sordid details of that fateful day and it could follow her the rest of her life. But how did they ever get started on Zeke? He gritted his teeth when it appeared Hobie was not willing to let it go.

It wasn't so much the sheriff's blunt questions about the man's obsession with Gracie that made Garth sick on his stomach, but her answers. It had taken a long time to forgive Zeke for taking advantage of Gracie while Garth was in the army hospital, but he was beginning to fear that he'd never heard the whole story. Did he really want to know?

He glared at his wife. She sucked in a deep breath and covered her face with her hands. "It's my fault. It's all my fault."

His stomach wrenched. Was she saying it was her fault that Ludie left or her fault that she hadn't told him the whole truth about her and Zeke? A vivid mental image of Zeke holding Gracie in his arms and kissing her lips caused Garth to shiver. He rubbed his temples as if he could massage away the heartbreaking images. He had to rebuke the vain imaginations invading his thoughts and destroying his trust. She'd never given him reason to distrust her. Knowing how hard it would be for her to reveal their last conversation with Ludie, he wasn't surprised when she broke down. "Honey, don't cry. Please don't cry. What happened was not your fault. You were a very good mother to Ludie."

"Thank you for that, Garth. But I'm getting so confused. I sit here and listen and wonder if things really happened the way Hobie says. Maybe I'm in denial."

Disappointed that Gracie was still dwelling on Hobie's ridiculous scenario, he regretted the promise he made to her before leaving home. Pointing fingers wouldn't bring Ludie home. All he wanted was to find her—to know that she was safe.

"Maybe I am a hypocrite. Have I twisted the truth in my own mind in order to live with myself?"

He leaned back and groaned. "No, sweetheart. You've done nothing to be ashamed of. Nothing!" For the past three years, Garth believed with all his heart that Gracie had been faithful to him while he was in the hospital. He didn't like the doubts now creeping into his thoughts. Rather than ignoring them, it was time to put the subject of Zeke Thorne to rest for both their sakes. "Honey, the man had hopes of marrying you. So?" Gesturing with his hand, he said, "Look at her, Hobie. What man wouldn't want to come home to such a sweet, beautiful wife? But it would've simply been a marriage of convenience, since she'd made it clear that she was still in love with me. She never gave him reason to believe she was in love with him."

The sheriff leaned forward in his chair. "Maybe he had a hard time believing that she was in love with a dead man."

"But I wasn't dead."

The sheriff's lip curled. "No, but neither Gracie nor Zeke knew that, and they were both young and very much alive. It's not out of reason to think Zeke might have become enraged when he learned of Ludie's attempts to break them up. Perhaps he made a vow to one day get even. We may be getting somewhere." Hobie reached across the table for his phone. Holding it to his ear, he said, "Pauline, I need you to run across the street to the Power Company and see if there is an address on Zeke . . .hold on." With his hand over the receiver, he said, "What's the fellow's last name?"

Garth felt a sense of relief when Gracie said, "Please hang up. This isn't getting us anywhere. Zeke did not kidnap Ludie."

The sheriff laid the phone back on the cradle and smiled. "Frankly, I didn't think he did. I was hoping if I could stir the two of you up, you'd finally tell me what you know, so we can figure out how to find her."

Gracie jumped up and ran out the door.

Garth stood and extended his hand. "Sorry, Hobie. I appreciate your time, but this has Gracie so upset, she's not been able to think straight. The truth has been hard to face."

****

Clementine waited until she was confident everyone was asleep before picking up her bag and slipping out the door. She searched the yard in the moonlight until she found an empty snuff can. Perfect! Taking the knife and spoon from her knapsack, she punched two tiny holes in the can, then dug through the rich, black dirt near the back steps until she found five nice-sized wigglers. After filling the can with worms and dirt, she stuffed the Red Rooster can in her pocket and walked toward the woods. A sadness filled her heart. How she wished she could stay. As much as she resented the Pearl woman's harsh words, she couldn't deny there was truth in what she said. It wouldn't be right to burden such a nice family with her problems. Just as she reached the woods, she turned and looked back. Tears filled her eyes. She'd made so many mistakes but it was no time to dwell on what could've been.

****

Carly arose at dawn the following morning and after putting wood in the stove to cook breakfast, she walked out on the porch to awaken her guest. Her mouth gaped open, seeing the covers neatly folded at the foot of the empty cot. She ran in the bedroom, where Coop was standing over the wash basin, shaving.

"Coop, put on a shirt. She's gone. We've got to go find her."

He laid down the razor. "Honey, you've been a nervous wreck lately. There's no need to panic. I'm sure she woke up early and is playing outside on the swing."

"Not Emma. Ludie."

His face showed his disgust. "For crying out loud, Carly. She's a big girl. Apparently her own folks couldn't keep her penned in. I don't know why you'd feel you'd have more influence over her than they would. The girl's wild. Let her be."

"You sound so callous. Have you forgotten she saved Emma's life?"

"No, but neither have I forgotten that wild animals don't like to be penned in."

"She's not wild. She's a scared, sweet girl and I intend to find her and bring her home."

"Home? Honey, you're not making sense. This isn't her home, she's—"

Carly didn't stick around to hear the remainder of his sentence.

Coop's jaw tightened when he heard the door slam. He splashed water over his face, then grabbed his shirt from off the bedpost. He peeked in on Emma, who was sleeping soundly, and went to the backdoor, looking for his wife. Of all mornings for her to take off without fixing his breakfast, it would be today when he needed to be at work early.

"Stubborn woman!" He walked to the edge of the woods and called, but Carly was not in sight. The sun had not yet risen, and it was hard to see his hand in front of his face. He almost wished he'd never told her the girl in the swamps had saved their Emma. Carly appeared ridiculously obsessed with the waif, as if it were her duty to become the girl's servant for the remainder of her days. But he realized even if he hadn't told his wife, Emma would have, which still baffled him. How in tarnation could Emma relate such specific details since she was unconscious from the time she was pulled from the water? His mind replayed the horrible scenario as he pushed his way through the brush.

Torn between going on to the work site or finding Carly, his anger quickly turned to fear. She undoubtedly had become lost in the swamp. He attempted to console himself with the belief that she'd eventually find her way out, now that the sun was breaking through the darkness. Yet, the thought of her frightened while wandering alone in the dark, made him ashamed he'd spoken so harshly to her, earlier. Was it her fault she had a heart of gold and wanted to help every living creature under the sun? Wasn't that one of the things he loved about her? He recalled how she ignored her own health and went to help little Emma before they were married. A mother couldn't have done more, and if not for Carly, he had no doubt Emma would've died from Scarlet Fever.

He stopped short and listened when he heard the rustling of leaves up ahead. "Carly? Is that you, Carly?"

Clementine stepped out from behind a tree. "It's me, Mr.

Flanigan."

"Where's my wife?"

"Miz Flanigan?"

Doing nothing to hide his disgust, he said, "I believe that would be my wife. Have you seen her?"

"This morning?"

"Yes, this morning. Confound you, girl, she ran out of the house to find you, and now she's apparently lost. I've got to find her. I can't leave her out here alone, and I need to be at work."

"I'm sorry, sir. I didn't mean to cause no trouble. Why would she want to find me? I didn't take nothing. Honest! Is Emma with her?"

Cooper ran his hands through his hair. "Emma?" He swallowed hard. "No." He suddenly realized if Emma woke up and found them gone, she could leave the house to find them. Wouldn't the river be the first place she'd go? His heart hammered at the possibility of her sliding down the slippery bank and being carried away by the current. Should he continue searching for Carly, or rush back home to be with Emma? The fellow from the brickyard was to arrive at the job site with a load of bricks for the front steps. If he wasn't there to pay him, he'd leave. This was all Carly's fault. If she hadn't brought the girl home with her, none of this would be happening.

She said, "Mr. Flanigan, would you like for me to go back to the house and be there for Emma when she wakes up?"

Though he felt the burden lift from his shoulders, he didn't want to give the girl reason to feel he was beholden to her. After all, none of this would've happened if she'd—. Cooper sucked in a heavy breath. If she had what? If she hadn't been at the river to save Emma? If she had refused Carly's insistence to go eat a good meal? She was young, but not stupid. If she had left after supper? She tried, but Carly wouldn't hear of it. He rubbed his hand over the back of his neck. No, he couldn't blame her. If anyone was to be blamed it would be Carly for being such a softie. He caught his bottom lip between his teeth. Would he want her to be any other way? Seeing the girl was waiting for his answer, he nodded. "Yes, thank you. I think that would be wise."

She turned to walk away when Cooper called out. "Wait! Are you sure you know how to find your way back?"

Her smile was proof enough that she knew those swamps perhaps better than he did, which made him wander how long the girl had been squatting on his land? Not that it mattered at this point. Still, he wondered.

It must've been fifteen, perhaps even twenty minutes later when he heard the sobs. Before he could call out, Carly shouted his name. Running toward her, he grabbed her in his arms and held tightly. "Hey, it's okay. You're safe."

She tried to explain why she left and how she became turned around in the dense swamp. Her crying ceased when she learned Clementine was home with Emma. "I know you must be furious with me, but I can explain."

His lip curled in a wry smile. "I'll wait until tonight to be furious. Come on, let's get you back to the house."

"Coop, I know you wanted to be at work early. Now, that it's light, and I know Clementine is at home with Emma, I can find my way back. Everything looked so different in the dark."

His raised brow gave evidence that he wasn't as confident as she was. "Why don't you walk with me to the new house. It's less than a half-mile from here and I have a load of bricks coming this morning. I'm afraid the driver will leave if I'm not there to pay him. You can easily find your way home from there."

"A half-mile, you say?" Carly was surprised to discover she'd walked in circles and was much closer to the house than she could've imagined.

Just as they were in view of the new house, Cooper ran and yelled at the driver of a truck, which was pulling away. "Yo, Frank. Don't leave." He motioned for his men to stop what they were doing to help unload.

Carly said, "Coop, Clementine has come to our aid once again. I've been thinking that we should ask her to—"

"Excuse me, darling, but I need to catch Frank before he takes off." He ran toward the moving truck.

Her shoulders sagged. "Sure! We'll talk when you get home."

CHAPTER 11

How is it that the right words are never there when you need them, but always come forth with such clarity after the fact? Carly regretted that she didn't take the opportunity to come out and explain to Cooper her wish to take Clementine Graham into their home. It would've been the perfect time, since he was in a sympathetic mood when he found her wandering in the woods.

She could've rightly explained that it would be cruel and un-Christian to send the poor defenseless girl out into a cruel, hard world to fend for herself, and surely he would've agreed. Of course, he would have. She ventured there weren't many men as compassionate as Cooper Flanigan. Besides, he never refused her of anything he felt she really wanted.

Carly thought about all the opportunities she had growing up. There was always food on the table and a roof over her head. She recalled eating Sunday dinners at Mama and Papa Dobbs house. No one could cook like Mama Dobbs, but food always tastes better when served with love. Did Clementine deserve anything less?

Carly could hardly wait to get home and see her girls. *My girls.* She smiled. Without one, she would not have the other. As she approached the house, her heart sank seeing Pearl Greene sitting in the swing with Emma in her lap. Stepping up the pace, she yelled, "Where's Clementine?" As she drew closer, she saw Emma's little balled fist, wiping away tears. The child sailed out of Pearl's lap and ran toward Carly with open arms. "Aunt Pearl made her leave."

"What do you mean, made her leave?"

Pearl gave a slight chuckle. "Now, punkin, you know Aunt Pearl didn't make her do anything. We merely discussed her options and the girl seemed to agree when I suggested it was time for her to grow up and stop scrounging off folks. I told her—in love, of course—that she was old enough to get a job, and stop expecting other people to take care of her. To tell the truth, I think she appreciated the advice."

Carly stood with her mouth open, unable to believe what she was hearing. However, it wasn't at all surprising that Pearl felt the need to precede her comments with "to tell the truth, since so much of what came out of her mouth was questionable. "Tell me, Pearl. Where did you propose for her to get a job?"

"Naturally, I gave a couple of options. The washhouse doesn't pay much, but at least she could take pride in knowing she wasn't freeloading off good, hard-working families like yours. And in time, if she worked hard and saved her money, perhaps she'd be able to afford another dress or two and could apply for a better paying job at the mill."

Carly's jaw jutted forward. What she was about to say was not suitable for young ears. "Emma, sweetheart, Mama would like for you to go to your room and play while Pearl and I have a grown-up conversation."

Emma wiped her nose on her sleeve and smiled. "Are you mad at Aunt Pearl, too?"

"Yes, sweetheart. I'm furious with Aunt Pearl, too. Now, you run play."

After Emma left, Pearl said, "Frankly, I'm surprised at you, Carly. If you'll recall, I was in Coop and Emma's life before you ever knew they existed. To place the child in a situation where she has to choose between us is cruel and unfair."

"Choose between us? Are you delusional? I'm her mother. You're a family acquaintance. There's no choosing to be done."

****

Clementine followed the river, and when she was sure she'd gone far enough not to be found, she came upon a hollowed out spot near the bank, not big enough to pass for a cave, but at least large enough to add a bit of protection from the weather, should it rain.

She walked down to the river's edge, near a waterfall. The sound of the rushing water was comforting, and Clementine felt she could stay there forever. It was perfect! The clump of reeds growing nearby would provide a perfect fishing pole. She'd always loved fish and was sure she would never tire of either catching or eating them.

****

After spending time in the swamps Clementine was tired. Tired of sleeping on the ground, tired of being cold, and tired of being alone. She had enjoyed the muscadines, but there were no longer any left on the vines, and she'd eaten fish until she was afraid she'd grow gills. She had developed a taste for frog legs, but crickets, not so much. If only she had money, she'd go home. Her Grandpa George would lecture her about running away but he'd take her in, and love her just the same. She wasn't so sure about Garth and Gracie. After the way she acted, she couldn't blame them if they never wanted to see her again. She couldn't blame them if they wished they had never adopted her. Was it possible to un-adopt?

Her stomach growled, and she could almost smell Grandpa's delicious Brunswick stew. What she'd give for a big bowl tonight.

After digging for earthworms, she thrust a hook into the biggest, fattest, most aggressive one. As many times as she'd done it, she still cringed, seeing the worm writhing as the sharp hook pierced his body. "Sorry, Mr. Worm. But it's you or me." The hook barely hit the water when she felt a tug on the line and pulled in a nice-sized bream. She opened the box of matches in her knapsack and winced, seeing so few left. Perhaps she should've paid more attention when studying about how the Indians rubbed rocks together to make fire. She gutted the fish, then cooked it over a fire the way she and Garth had done many times.

She spread the blanket on the ground and lay down. Gazing into the sky at the fluffy clouds, shifting into various shapes, she saw the outline of a chicken. Or was it a duck? Before she could determine, the clouds moved, forming new shapes. Clementine blinked and blinked again. There was no chicken, no duck . . . just a distinct pair of angel wings directly over her.

A verse from Psalms popped in her head. "I will give the angels charge over thee to protect thee in all thy ways." If the angels were really watching over her, why was she out here, all alone, with winter coming and no food? Feeling ashamed, she shifted her thinking. Didn't God give her a fish when she was hungry? True, he didn't cause it to jump out of the water into the fire, but he'd given her everything she needed to catch the fish. He provided the worm. She found herself singing a song she'd heard at church. *"Alas and did my Savior bleed . . . Would He devote that sacred head, for such a worm as I?"* She stopped singing. "That's me. A worm."

She lay down on the blanket and pulled it around her. *What a fine fix you've got yourself into.* With winter fast approaching, there was no way she could continue to live outdoors in the cold, Georgia mountains. After mulling over her situation, Clementine concluded she had to find a way to get money for a bus ticket to South Alabama. Once there, as difficult as it would be, she'd need to muster up the courage to confess her shameful sin to Garth and Gracie. It would be the hardest thing she'd ever done, but she had to know if she'd committed the unpardonable sin and they knew about things like that. But even if her sin wasn't the one God couldn't forgive, would she be considered a marked woman forever for sharing her bed with a fellow who wasn't her husband? She pulled her wedding ring from her change purse, and wondered it she could possibly sell it for bus money.

Why did she always hurt the ones who loved her most? Three years ago, she'd left Grandpa George and Gracie when she ran away. Though she was undeserving of their forgiveness when she returned, they loved her as if she'd done no wrong. And when she met Schooner, didn't Garth, Gracie and Grandpa, even having never met him, warn her that she was making a mistake? If only she had listened. Was it right to expect them to forgive her after the horrible things she said before leaving? Did she honestly think they'd want to see her?

But they weren't the only ones she had wronged. Why did she allow conniving Pearl Greene to cause her to run off the way she did, without waiting to thank the Flanigans' for the kindness bestowed upon her? It was rude and inexcusable. She couldn't leave Cartersville without apologizing to them for her behavior.

****

She had forgotten how far she walked the day she left the Flanigan's before arriving at her campsite. The sun had gone down before Clementine reached Carly and Cooper's house. She stood approximately a hundred feet away, holding her knapsack in front of her with both hands and staring at the peaceful scene. The lights in the house had a warm glow. Smoke from the wood stove rose in gentle puffs. Rubbing her arms, she shivered from the cool night air. She could almost feel the love inside from where she stood.

A chill ran down her spine. What would it have been like if things had turned out the way she'd so desperately wished? But because of her foolish rebellion, she had refused to listen to wise counsel. It was all her fault. She made her bed and now she'd have to sleep in it. She almost found the old adage humorous. What bed? She didn't even have a bed nor money to buy one. The gruesome thought almost made her turn around and run back into the woods. She could see Carly through the kitchen window, standing over the stove. As she drew closer, the smell of ham cooking filled her nostrils. She had no right to impose. If Carly should offer supper, she'd pretend not to be hungry.

She knocked on the door, and when no one came, she almost turned around and walked away. Just as she was about to leave, the front door flew open and Emma ran and sailed into her arms. "I knew you'd come back. I told Mama not to worry."

Carly and Cooper appeared, and greeted her as if she were their very own prodigal daughter. Carly said, "Emma is right. She never gave up that you'd be back. I'm happy she was right. Come on in. We're just about to serve supper."

Clementine shook her head. "Thank you, ma'am, but I had a big meal before I left." Then fearing she'd lied, she retracted. "Well, a fairly big meal." Smiling, she added. "Well, the fish was about this big, but quite satisfying at the time."

Cooper laughed. "My wife always cooks as if she's cooking for a crowd. I assure you there is more than we can eat on the table. Please, come in and let's eat."

Clementine stopped short, seeing a strange fellow at the table stand as she entered. She tipped her head, acknowledging his presence. "I'm sorry. I didn't know you had company. I'll be moving on. I just wanted to stop by and thank you folks for all you did for me. I reckon you're about the nicest people I've ever had the privilege of knowing. I won't never forget you, as long as I live." She wrung her hands together. "Well, I reckon that's about it."

Carly wrapped her arms around her. "Oh, no, you don't. I insist you take your place at this table." Then cutting her eyes toward the young man, she said, "Clementine, this is Johnny McLanders. He's here in view of a call, and will be staying with us until after the voting takes place, tomorrow."

She had no idea what it meant to view a call, but did it matter? She'd be moving on shortly. He looked like a decent sort of fellow—but for all Clementine knew, he could be a dirty-rotten scoundrel. It was apparent that her ability to judge one's character was lacking, else she would never have left town with Schooner. A sharp, gnawing pain rose from the pit of her stomach. She wanted to hate Schooner for the horrifying trick he pulled on her. He was cruel and heartless. Her good name was blighted the moment he crawled into her bed. She could never marry. Ever. If she confessed her shame to her husband-to-be, he wouldn't want her. If she didn't tell, the truth would be bound to come out after they were married, and her husband's pride would demand he divorce her on the grounds that she deceived him. It wouldn't matter to him that Schooner only kissed her . . . her bed was defiled the moment Schooner crawled under the covers.

Cooper blessed the food and as soon as he uttered "Amen," Emma blurted, "Where did you go, Clemmie?" Then looking over at Carly, she quickly added. "Sorry. None of my business. Right, Mama?"

Carly tucked a napkin under Emma's collar. "You're learning, dear. That's exactly right. No more questions at the table."

Carly and Cooper did most of the talking that evening, since Clementine didn't appear eager to share much about her past. And Johnny wasn't adding to the conversation. The thought ran through Carly's mind that he might not be as bashful as he appeared, but seeing the way his gaze would linger on Clementine, perhaps he was smitten by her beauty. From all appearances, Clementine had made no preparations for her future, but she was young and with her looks, it shouldn't be difficult for her to find a good husband to take care of her. What horrible set of circumstances had led such a sweet girl to wind up with no home and no hope?

Carly stared into the beautiful, yet sunken eyes. It was obvious she'd not had much sleep. Did it really matter where she was from or what led to such dire circumstances? She would no longer be homeless or hopeless. For the first time since losing the baby, Carly found herself eager for Cooper to finish the big farmhouse.

Clementine could have her very own room. Tomorrow, they'd go shopping for a new dress. They'd take her to church and introduce her into the community, where she could meet the right boy. But first, she'd need to convince Coop that Clementine was not there by coincidence. God had brought her to them and they had an obligation to help her.

After supper, Johnny excused himself to go to his car to bring in his suitcase. Carly suggested Clementine might like to put Emma to bed and tell her a story. It was difficult to determine which one appeared to like the idea the most as they held hands and giggled all the way to Emma's bedroom. It gave Carly the perfect opportunity to present her plan to Cooper.

His gaze locked with hers. Moisture welled in her big green eyes as she waited for his answer. Drawing a deep breath, he said, "Honey, I've prayed for a long time for the Lord to deliver you from the deep pit you seem to have fallen into. I haven't seen you this happy since . . . well, what I'm trying to say is that it's good to see the light return to your eyes. Of course, she can stay. But she's a teenager, and we must treat her with the same love, guidance and discipline that we'd give if we were her parents."

"I understand, but don't be too harsh on her, Coop. After being alone and responsible for making her own decisions, I'm sure it'll be an adjustment to have someone usurping her authority."

Cooper rubbed his hand across the back of his neck, a nervous habit of his when he didn't know which way to turn. However, he had no intention of arguing with Carly. When her mind was made up, even a bulldozer couldn't sway her. If his fears had merit, it wouldn't take long for the truth to come out. He couldn't conceive of a parent kicking a child out of the house with little more than the clothes on her back without a very good reason. He conceded he'd known a few adults in his lifetime who weren't fit to raise a kid, but he had a suspicion that wasn't the case with Miss Eliza Clementine Graham. She was courteous and appeared to have been taught proper manners, a sign of good parenting.

Though she had earlier portrayed herself as an orphan, he wondered if it was a ploy to keep from being sent home. Surely, there were heartbroken parents somewhere who at this very moment were frantically searching for their beloved daughter. A lump forming in his throat made it hard to swallow. Perhaps the girl was *too* beloved. Spoiled, maybe? How many times had he said it was impossible to love a child too much? Maybe he was wrong.

His emotions rocked back and forth in roller-coaster fashion, with frightening ups and downs. With no concrete reason to insist the girl leave or insist that she stay, he threw up his hands. What could it hurt to humor Carly and provide the girl food and shelter until they could learn more about why she'd resorted to hiding out in the woods? He answered his own question: Emma was young and impressionable and a runaway teen that he knew nothing about could have an adverse effect on his little girl. He had ample reason to worry. But what was Clementine Graham afraid of?

CHAPTER 12

Garth and Gracie were eating at the Diner, when Sheriff Hobie walked in the door. He moseyed over to their table. After an awkward exchange of meaningless chit-chat about the weather and the daily special, Garth asked if he might like to join them.

Gracie said, "Hobie, it was rude of me to leave in such a huff, yesterday, but it's been hard for me to face the truth. I wanted you to help us find Ludie, yet there are details concerning her disappearance, which I haven't wanted to disclose."

"I suspected there was more to this situation than meets the eye. Suppose you two stop beating around the bush and tell me exactly what's going on here. That is, if you really want to find your missing ward."

Garth bit his lip, and waited for the fireworks, knowing most assuredly that the sheriff's blunt comment would cause a volcanic-like eruption in Gracie. He watched as her brows knitted together.

Then, raising her hand, she pointed her index finger so close to the sheriff's nose that Garth suspected she could feel his breath on her hand,

"Hobie Fowler, I'll have you know Ludie is not a missing ward. She's our daughter."

The sheriff's face blushed. "Begging your pardon, Gracie. I do recall you saying y'all had adopted her, but it slipped my mind. I was just remembering her from years ago when we were trying to locate her. She was a ward back then, I believe—not that it matters. Naturally, even if she were one of the wards, I'd still want to give the situation my full attention. But it will help if you'll be completely honest with why she left."

"Thank you. Apology accepted."

The waitress brought in their food, and Garth relaxed when the tense conversation ceased. But just as they finished eating, Gracie turned to her husband. "Garth, would you like to tell him what we know?"

"Are you sure?" After she nodded, he gazed up at the ceiling, as if trying to decide where to begin."

"Hobie, it's true Ludie was a handful when she first came to us. I was away fighting the war at the time, but Ludie would write me of all her little shenanigans." He smiled as if the memory was a fond one.

"Shenanigans? So, I suppose by the time she arrived at the orphanage, she was already out of control."

Gracie shook her head. "No. She's always been a strong-willed child, but at the same time, she wants desperately to please."

"I don't understand. Were you able to contol her or not?"

"Of course we could control her. She had her own opinions, which couldn't be shaken, but she was never disobedient. Never!"

When he smirked, Gracie reached for Garth's hand. "This isn't working. Let's go."

Hobie didn't seem to have a clue what had just happened, but it was evident this time she was serious about leaving. Suited him fine. He had more important things to do rather than waste time trying to find a sixteen-year-old girl who apparently chose to take off. Besides, at sixteen, she was old enough to decide whether she wanted to leave or stay.

"I hope that if she returns, to the orphanage, that she'll understand the heartache she's caused you, and will settle down and behave herself. On the other hand, if she doesn't return on her own, but you happen to locate her, I pray you'll make the right decision, whether to leave her or make her return with you. Sorry, we couldn't see eye-to-eye on this. Good luck."

Garth shook his hand and thanked him for sparing his time.

On the way home, Garcie said, "Did you hear what he said?"

Garth was slow to answer, knowing there was no right or wrong answer. He wanted nothing more than to leave the past forty-five minutes behind, rather than rehash all the things that Gracie had found offensive. "Yes, dear, I think I heard everything."

"Then you heard him when he indicated if we found her, we'd have to *make* her come home. Make her. That's the very words he used."

"Uh . . . yes, I believe he did. But hon, you'll have to admit he has more reason to suspect Ludie is a wayward teen than to think something nefarious has happened to her. I'm afraid if we were on the outside looking in, we might be of the same opinion."

She shrugged. "Maybe."

"We probably should've stayed and told him the whole story. I thought that was what you had intended to do."

"I did, but I couldn't bring myself to do it, Garth. We know what she did and we love her still. But I'm sure if others who don't know her should hear what happened before she left, they wouldn't see her in the same light that we see her. "Right or wrong, she's still our sweet Ludie." The tears that had been puddling in her eyes, were now trickling down her cheeks. "We have to find her, Garth. I can't eat or sleep until I know if she's safe and happy.. If she is, I won't insist that she come home."

He pulled her closer and kissed the top of her head. "We'll find her. I promise."

CHAPTER 13

Clementine walked back into the sitting room and blushed when Johnny stood as she entered—the same way he did when she'd entered the dining room—as if she were someone special. If he only knew the truth. But as shy as he was, there was little chance he'd ever know anything about any girl. She'd never known such a bashful fellow.

Carly said, "Please join us dear."

Clementine picked up her knapsack sitting near the fireplace. "You've got a really sweet little girl. Emma went right off to sleep after the story."

Carly beamed. "I'm sure she'll have sweet dreams tonight. It's easy to see she adores you. Thank you, Clementine."

"It was my pleasure, ma'am." She glanced over at the fellow they called Johnny, standing in the corner, chewing on a toothpick. He made her nervous the way he stared as if he could see straight through her. She could hardly talk without stuttering. She had a mind to come out and ask him why he was looking at her that way. Even when she wasn't viewing him out of the corner of her eye, she could feel his eyes focused on her. "Uh . . .uh, ma'am, I didn't come intending to eat, but I sure appreciate the delicious supper. Don't know when I've tasted anything as good as your corned beef hash. I wanted to come by and thank you folks for treating me with such kindness. You had a right to notify the law and have me arrested for trespassing on your property, but I'm mighty grateful that you didn't. Well, that's what I come to say, so I reckon I'll be moving on."

Johnny said, "May I walk you to your car?"

"Car? I ain't got no car."

"Then may I drive you where you need to go?"

"Where I need to go?" Did he mean jail? "I hope not."

He scratched his head. "I'm sorry. I didn't mean to offend you."

"I'm sorry, that came out wrong. What I meant to say was that I have plans to leave town to go back where I came from."

Carly spoke up quickly, "It's still quite early, Clementine. Surely, you can stay a little longer. Why don't you and Johnny go sit on the porch and get acquainted, and I'll bring you a cup of hot apple cider."

Johnny said, "Thank you, I'd like that—that is, if Miss Graham doesn't mind."

Clemmie could see what Carly was doing, and she wasn't at all interested in starting up a courtship—now, or ever again.

Assuming it would be humiliating to Johnny, and rude to Carly to refuse such a simple request, she feigned a smile. "Sharing a cup of cider on the porch with good company sounds appealing but I can't stay long."

Carly's eyes lit up, as if she'd won a prize.

Clemmie sat down in the swing and though there were two chairs on the porch, Johnny walked over and sat beside her. Surprising for someone so shy. After an awkward silence, she attempted to carry on a one-way conversation with boring small-talk about the weather, boiled peanuts, and how beautiful the cotton fields were back home. What was wrong that a twenty-something-year-old man couldn't carry on a simple conversation? Clemmie didn't know whether to be furious or to feel sorry for him. With hopes of either drawing him out of his timidity or preferably sending him back into the house, she clapped her palm over her lips and gasped. "Oh, m'goodness, how I do go on. I've been a real chatterbox. I'd love to hear your thoughts." Now it was up to him. She was done.

Almost as if he'd been waiting for her to stop rattling on, he responded softly.

"Clementine! Beautiful. I love it."

Her brow shot up. The creaking of the swing grew louder. Did this fellow she'd known less than an hour and who had said less than a half-dozen words just tell her she was beautiful *and* that he was in love with her? Absurd. Not that she didn't believe in love at first sight, since she'd never forget the way her heart hammered the day she met Schooner on the bridge. But that was different. Wasn't it? She wanted to ask him to repeat what he said, but wouldn't it be better to drop the subject, to keep from embarrassing both of them? When curiosity became stronger than her will, she mumbled, "I beg your pardon?" Her pulse raced as she waited.

When his gaze locked with hers, his lip turned up in a wry smile. She quickly glanced away, which must've strengthened his nerve, for his lovely baritone voice belted out a catchy little tune. "Oh, my darling, Oh, my darling, Clementine."

She smiled, recalling Mrs. Flanigan telling her about a song called Clementine. Had her mother heard it before she was born? Johnny must've sang every verse. Or had he sung the same verse several times? She licked her dry lips and tried to discern if she was relieved to learn he was speaking of the song being beautiful, or a mite disappointed that the compliment wasn't directed at her. Not that she'd ever be interested in him, but at such a low point in her life, she could certainly use a kind word to lift her low spirits.

She jumped up and the swing jerked. "Sorry, but I should go."

"Did I embarrass you?"

Her voice quaked. "Embarrass me? Of course not, but I have to make plans. Did I tell you I intend to return to Alabama?" The minute the words left her lips, she cringed. She didn't owe him an explanation of her goings and comings, nor had he indicated he expected one.

"I'm really sorry to hear you're leaving. I'll forever be singing the lyrics, "You are lost and gone forever, dreadful sorrow,

Clementine."

She relaxed, now that his dry sense of humor was showing, though the lyrics made her feel a little sad. Even though she felt lost and gone forever from everyone's life whom she'd ever cared about, it was doubtful that anyone other than Grandpa George was dreadfully sorry at her absence. She mustered up a smile, seeing Johnny waiting for her response.

"That's sweet, Johnny, but if you really knew me, you wouldn't be sorry to see me go."

He smiled. "Oh, but you're wrong. Do you mind if I write to you?"

She shrugged. "I reckon that would be all right, if you really want to." She hoped he wouldn't press her, since she had no idea how or when she'd get back to Goat Hill. She only knew she would—somehow, someway, someday.

"I'll walk you inside and get something for you to write your address on."

She hesitated when he handed her a small pad and a pen. She wrote down Grandpa George's address, since that's where she intended to go. *Clementine Graham, Route 3, Goat Hill, Alabama, c/o George—* She ripped out the sheet and tore it up. Grandpa George would get her goat if she had her mail sent to his cottage. Gossip of the white orphan the Grahams raised, living in the tenant shack back of the Nine Gables Orphanage would be all over Goat Hill before the Postman could get back to the Post Office.

She took another page from the writing pad and penned, "Miss

Ludie Graham, c/o Nine Gables Orphanage, Goat Hill, Alabama."
Grandpa George usually took the mail in the house for Gracie, and
Clemmie would be sure to tell him to watch for any mail addressed
to her and slip it in his pocket. Not that she really expected Johnny
to write. He barely knew her. It was probably a line he used on all
the girls, but it wouldn't be the first time a fellow lied to her.
Didn't matter to her if he never wrote. It wasn't her idea.

Johnny looked at the address and frowned. "Ludie? Who's
Ludie?"

"That's me. My full name is Elizabeth Clementine Graham,
and folks there call me Ludie."

"I see! Well, I hope you don't mind if I still call you
Clementine, even if I do address your letters to Ludie?"

"That's fine.".

They walked into the living room, where they found Carly
knitting and Cooper reading the paper.

Johnny gazed at the address, and smiled, as if she'd handed
him a prized document. "Clementine. I'd be happy to take you
wherever you need to go, if you'd let me."

Carly said, "Oh, my goodness, I promised you apple cider. I
forgot. It'll only take a minute."

Clemmie shook her head. "Please don't bother. It's time I
moved on."

Johnny said, "I need to go look over my notes for tomorrow.
Goodnight, all." He reached for Clemmie's hand and kissed the
back of it. "It was a pleasure to make your acquaintance, Miss

Clementine. I hope we can meet again, sometime."

Carly said, "Don't forget—we'll expect you back here for breakfast in the morning."

"Thank you, ma'am. I'll be here."

After he left the room, Carly motioned to Cooper with a slight toss of her head. She whispered, "Tell her. Go ahead. Tell her."

He nodded. "Uh, Clementine, Carly and I have been talking, and we'd like—"

Just as he figured, Carly interrupted, eager to tell it. "What my husband is trying to say is that we would very much like to have you make this your home. We have plenty of room." Carly had expected her to be elated, yet the expression on her face was not one of joy, but of confusion.

"Why would you do that? You don't know anything about me." The rise in her voice almost sounded as if she resented the offer.

"I've had a feeling that, for whatever reason, you aren't eager to return to Alabama, but may feel you have no other option. We're saying you don't have to leave. Don't you want to stay?"

"It ain't that, ma'am. But I reckon if you knew my story, you'd be wary of getting involved with the likes of me."

Cooper sat quietly as he listened to the conversation. Carly might not be wary, but the idea was making him most uncomfortable. The girl had just admitted they were inviting trouble by taking her in under their roof. He rubbed the back of his neck. Observing the smile on his wife's face, he was only fooling himself if he thought there was anything he could do or say, which would change her mind. Not tonight, anyway.

"Then it's settled. I'll have your room on the screened porch ready in two shakes. Coop hooked up a shower just outside the back door, if you'd like to bathe before going to bed."

"Thank you. That would be nice. The trek here was long and dusty."

Carly followed Cooper to their bedroom, where she pulled extra bedcovers and a towel from the chifforobe.

****

Clemmie picked up her knapsack and walked to the corner of the house, to shower. She hadn't intended to eat supper and she certainly had no thoughts of staying overnight, but considering that it rained earlier and the ground was wet, a goodnight's sleep in a bed sounded too tempting to resist. But who were these people and what motive did they have for taking in a wayward girl, whom they knew nothing about. Was it the Flanigans' she didn't trust— or herself? They seemed genuine, but she admitted she hadn't been very good at judging character in the past.

Holding the linens, Carly stood on her tiptoes and kissed her husband. "You go on to bed, sweetheart. I'll be back, after I get Clemmie settled."

He whispered. "It's Clemmie, now, is it?"

"It's what Emma calls her, and if we're to be family, perhaps we should, too. It sounds less formal than Clementine, don't you think?"

"Family?"

The question didn't require an answer. Carly couldn't discern if his frown was evidence that he didn't approve of the nickname or if he was opposed to her referring to the poor, sweet, homeless girl as "family." Whatever the case, he was a compassionate man and it wouldn't take long for him to come around to her way of thinking.

With a hand on either side of Carly's cheeks, he kissed her once more. "You have a big heart, darling. You won't be long, will you?"

"Not too long, but don't bother to wait up. Clemmie and I have a lot to talk about."

Carly had the bed made and the covers pulled back by the time Clemmie finished showering.

"Thank you, ma'am. The shower was refreshing. You and your husband have been too kind."

The curiosity was almost more than Carly could stand. "Honey, you are welcome here as long as you wish to stay. I hope you won't think I'm trying to meddle when I say what I'm about to say. But I'd love to get to know you better, and I feel you deserve to know more about us. Why don't we sit outside on the steps to talk, so we don't disturb Coop and Emma?"

Waiting for neither consent nor disapproval, and fearing the latter, Carly opened the door and sat on the steps. Pressing forward, she said, "I'll go first and tell you something about me. I was born and raised not too far from here, in Cobb County. My father owned a hot dog stand that boasted of being the 'Best hot dogs in the world.' Now, I'm not sure that was ever proven, but I can attest to the fact they were the best I had ever eaten. I don't suppose it counts that my daddy's hot dogs were the only hot dogs I'd ever had. At sixteen, I fell in love with a handsome young fellow at Cartersville High, by the name of Julian Dugan." Her eyes filled with moisture. "We were so in love, we quit school and ran away to get married. We didn't have two nickels to rub together, but we were too much in love to realize how poor we really were."

Carly chuckled at the fond memory, leaving Clemmie confused. Her eyes squinted. "But you call your husband—"

"Coop! Cooper Flanigan. Yes." Carly's voice lowered to a whisper. "I love Coop with all my heart, but there's something about that first love that one never forgets. One day, dear, you'll understand what I'm saying."

"Yes ma'am."

"Well, Julian got a job working in the sawmill in Cartersville, and we moved into this very house, although it was only one room at the time and in bad need of repair. We were so happy, back then and it wasn't long before I learned I was pregnant." Her chin quivered. "We were poor, but we were living off love. Then one day, our world turned upside down when Julian lost an arm in an accident at the sawmill. Almost overnight he became bitter and difficult to live with. Of course, I knew he was worried about me, but it didn't make him any easier to live with."

"So I suppose you divorced?"

"Oh, no. Although life had become very difficult, I loved him and would never have left. One day, I received a letter from a former neighbor who had moved to a little place called Marl, in South Alabama. She insisted that we move to Marl and live with them until we could get on our feet. Her husband owned a feed store, but Pearl—you met Pearl—said they were planning to buy a dairy and would need someone to run the store for them. They offered the job to Julian."

"Yes'm, I met her and right off I got the distinct feeling your friend Miz Pearl didn't like me."

"Sugar, Pearl doesn't like anyone who has nothing to offer her."

"Maybe it ain't right for me to say it, ma'am, but I'm glad you didn't go to Marl, or I would never have met you and your family."

"Oh, but we did go."

"But, you still live in Cartersville . . . and Miz Pearl, too." With her head slightly cocked, she lifted her hands, palms out. "I'm confused."

"It's a long story. Julian—my first husband—and I had never met Cooper, but he lived in Cartersville and we learned from Pearl that he was wanting to get to Marl. Cooper didn't have a car and we needed a driver, so he drove us to Alabama in Julian's truck. We arrived at Ed and Pearl's house in Marl in the middle of the night, but things didn't turn out the way she promised."

"That's too bad. Your husband didn't get the job?"

"Not only that—Pearl pretended she never invited us to stay with them. Julian became deathly ill with gangrene on the trip, yet she left us standing at the front door, claiming she never wrote such a letter. I couldn't believe what was happening. I was sure Cooper didn't believe me, but I didn't have the letter to prove she was lying."

"Goodness, that's awful. Bless your heart."

"I'll be okay. It just makes my blood boil, though when I think about what poor Julian went through that night."

"Is it possible he could've been saved, if she would've invited you in and called a doctor?"

"I'll never know. Probably not, but at least I wouldn't live with that agonizing question looming in the back of my mind."

"It's a shame your husband didn't live to see his little girl. Emma's a doll."

"She's a doll, all right, but Emma is Cooper's niece. His sister died a few years ago and he became Emma's guardian. Unfortunately, I lost my baby right after I lost Julian." She blew out a heavy breath before continuing. "Those were hard times. I was alone and stuck in a strange town. I needed a job, and Cooper needed a governess for Emma . . . and well, that's how it all began. Then three years ago—" Her voice cracked. "But enough about me. I'm eager to hear your story."

Clementine shook her head vigorously. "Nah, you wouldn't. It ain't pretty from start to finish." She lifted a shoulder in a shrug. "Well, I reckon it ain't finished yet, but it might as well be. I'm no good and don't reckon I ever have been."

"Sweetheart, you're young and beautiful with a long life ahead of you. We've all made mistakes in life, but those mistakes don't define who we are." She swallowed hard. How could she convince someone else it was truth if she couldn't believe it herself? Tell me what happened to make you want to live in the river swamp?"

"Want to? Is that what you think?" Her eyes glassed over. "But I got no right to complain, I made my bed and I reckon I have to sleep in it, even if it is on a riverbank. It ain't nobody's fault but my own, the way things turned out." Her voice cracked. "I had it real good before I got stupid and blew it.

"Suppose you start at the beginning."

"I ain't sure that's a good idea. Telling about my beginning is what got me where I am today."

Carly reached over and grasped her hand. "Well, if you're saying you have nothing more to lose, would you please share your story with me? I promise there's nothing you can say that can shock me and nothing you can reveal that will cause me to think less of you."

Clemmie bit her lip. The woman had been good to her and all she asked in return was an explanation of how she wound up in such dire straits. Didn't she owe her that much. Sucking in a lungful of air, then blowing out slowly, she nodded. "Just remember, you asked for it, but I won't hold you to it."

"I beg your pardon? You won't hold me to what?"

"You said you wouldn't think less of me after you learn who I really am."

"And I meant it. You've said you were raised in an orphanage. Let's begin there. Do you know who your parents are?"

"Yes'm. And I reckon if I start there, that'll make this a very short story, since you won't care nothing about knowing the rest."

Carly said, "You're wrong, sweetheart. But it's getting a bit chilly sitting on these concrete steps. Let's go inside, lie down on the cot and wrap up in the quilt. Wouldn't that be more comfortable?"

"I'm fine, ma'am. You take the quilt. I'll just sit here on the floor."

"Nonsense." She slid over on the cot and sat up with her back braced against the wall. Drawing the quilt over her knees, she said, "Crawl on up. There's plenty of room."

Clemmie remained plopped down on the floor with her knees bent and her arms wrapped around her legs. "No'm. It ain't right for me to let you keep giving and giving. I ain't worthy of such goodness."

"What are you talking about? That's ridiculous. God said you are worthy."

"He did?"

"Of course, he did. He said you are wonderfully and fearfully made—that he knew you even before he formed you in your mother's womb, and that he loves you very much. If that doesn't prove you're worthy, I don't know what it would take."

Clemmie yawned. "I wonder . . ."

"What, dear?"

"I wonder why . . . why would God love a baby in Comfort's womb?"

"What do you mean by a comfortable womb?"

"Don't mind me. I was just pondering. Miz Flanigan, do you mind if I go to sleep now? I'm dog-tired."

Carly tiptoed into her room and crawled into bed with her husband. "Coop . . . are you awake?"

"I wasn't, but I am now."

"Emma would love to have a sister, don't you think?"

"A sister? Honey, are you saying what I think you're saying?"

She laid her hand on his chest. "Then you aren't opposed?"

"Opposed? I'm thrilled. It's what I've been waiting to hear you say, but could we please finish the conversation later? It's after midnight."

"Of course. I just needed to know we both wanted the same thing. Goodnight, sweetheart."

CHAPTER 14

The following morning, Carly was singing *Buttons and Bows* while preparing breakfast. Johnny walked in and said, "My, you're in a chipper mood."

Coop eased up behind her as she stood at the stove and kissed her on the neck. He said, "I feel rather chipper, myself."

Clemmie was setting the table and Emma was right by her side. After everyone was seated, Carly said, "Johnny, would you mind blessing the food for us?"

After the prayer, Coop picked up the bacon platter to hand down the table, when Carly said, "Clemmie, Coop and I had a talk last night, and we agreed that we want you to become a part of our forever family. So any thoughts you have of going back to the orphanage can be forgotten. We want you here with us. Emma will be so thrilled to have you for a sister." She reached for Coop's hand and smiled. "Isn't that right dear?"

His Adam's apple bobbed a time or two. "Sister? Uh . . . that's what you mentioned last night?"

"Yes, it was. And Clemmie, just so you'll know, when I brought it up, Coop said it was what he'd been waiting to hear me say."

Emma seemed a little confused at first. But after allowing the words to sink in, she screeched, "Clemmie is my sister, now?"

Carly nodded. "Yes, dear. That is, if she accepts us as her family."

Johnny's gaze locked with Clemmie's. "I think that's wonderful. No one could ever wish for a better family."

Clemmie's thoughts were spinning. Johnny was right. The Flanigans' were wonderful. But she missed her own family. If only she could go back to the way things were before . . . before Schooner. But there was no going back. She'd ruined everything. Gracie and Garth could never forgive her for the harsh things she said before running away, and she couldn't blame them. Surely, Grandpa George felt she was just like her mama . . . bad to the bone. What else could he think? What made her any different? She left with the first guy who made a pass at her. Not only that, she shared her bed with him. Did she dare go back and face her grandpa? Even if he never said it, she'd always know what was in the back of his mind.

She glanced around the table, as all eyes were centered on her. Carly said, "Well, dear, what do you say? Will you join our little family and love us as much as we've learned to love you?"

Her chin quivered. "I don't know what to say . . . this has taken me by surprise. Are you really saying that you want me to—"

Carly nodded. "Yes! Yes, we want you to live with us. I'd like to get you enrolled in school, as soon as possible. What grade are you in, sweetheart?"

"I was in the eleventh grade, before I left."

"Well, I'm sure the Principal, Mr. Brooks will test you to place you where you need to be. We'll go shopping this afternoon and buy you some new clothes."

Clemmie wanted to shout, "No, no, I already have a family." But did she, really? She had just been presented with a wonderful offer. Wouldn't it be foolish not to accept?"

Johnny said, "If God makes way for me to pastor the Cartersville First Church tomorrow, it'll be good that I can see you instead of having to write, as we had planned."

Her thoughts scrambled. "A preacher? Is that what he meant when he spoke of 'a call?' He was a preacher? If it hadn't been so horrifying, it would've been funny. It wasn't hard to tell that he was smitten with her. If only he knew what she was hiding.

Saturday afternoon, Clemmie had little time to dwell on the past or the future. She was caught up in the here and now, as Carly drove her into Atlanta and bought an entire wardrobe. Emma hadn't let go of her hand since discovering she had a big sister.

That night, lying on the cot on the porch, Clemmie tossed and turned. She should be extremely happy that she wasn't out in the swamps, cold and possibly wet. Her stomach was full, and the people in this household thought she was wonderful. So why couldn't she be happy? She couldn't remember being this miserable when she was scrounging for food in the swamps.

Sunday morning, Johnny preached a wonderful sermon about a woman who went to a well to draw water. He said everyone in town looked down their nose at her. They all knew she'd allowed countless men into her bed . . . yet, Jesus came along, and told her she was forgiven . . . but not to do it, anymore. Johnny said when God forgives, He completely forgets about it, and that we should, too. If Jesus could forgive the woman at the well, who transgressed with many men, maybe He'd forgive her for her one transgression. Clemmie's heart beat so fast, she could hardly breathe. Never had she heard such a powerful sermon. Johnny spoke about being born again and when he encouraged anyone who needed to be born again to pray along with him, she did. Then, he ended his sermon by saying, "Go and sin no more."

We need to be born again! Go and sin no more. The words rolled around in her head. That's exactly what she'd do. Her life would begin from this very moment. It would be difficult to forget her past, but she'd work on it. If God was going to forget it, why shouldn't she? The hardest part about forgetting what she'd left behind would be forgetting Garth, Gracie and especially sweet ol' Grandpa George. But she would. She had to. Tears welled in her eyes.

It was almost as if Johnny were speaking directly to her, even though she knew he had no idea what she'd done. Perhaps it was God speaking to her through Johnny. He does that, doesn't he? Speak through preachers?

The church took a vote after the sermon, and unanimously voted to call Johnny as their pastor. Clemmie was convinced they made the right choice. Never had a sermon left her with such strong convictions.

Johnny went home with them for Sunday dinner, and said he'd be moving his things into the furnished Church Pastorium next door to the church, first thing Monday morning.

Clemmie hardly slept at all, Sunday night. She'd hoped the new Clemmie—the sinless, born-again Clemmie—would feel differently. She'd expected to have thoughts of those she left behind in Goat Hill to be wiped from her memory. They weren't. But what was worse, was the fact that wicked, evil, hard-hearted Schooner was still occupying her thoughts. Why couldn't she forget?

After dressing for school Monday morning, Carly oohed and ahhed over how Clemmie looked in her new school frocks. Although she would've preferred a much plainer dress than the frilly one Carly selected, she kept in mind that she wasn't the same, plain Clemmie that showed up in Cartersville. She had become new, and if that meant changing her looks, she'd go with it.

School went okay. The teacher was nice, and the students seemed excited to have a new pupil to join them. Everyone was nice, but there was one girl—Maurine—who was especially friendly.

CHAPTER 15

As much as Gracie had opposed sharing personal details leading up to Ludie's disappearance, after days of agonizing over it, she conceded with Garth that the only way they'd find their daughter would be to reveal the last heartbreaking conversation.

The sheriff didn't seem surprised to see them walk in.

Gracie had second thoughts the minute she saw the wry smile stretch across his face, but she was determined to carry through.

He said, "I suppose you're now ready to stop whatever it is you're hiding? What is it that I need to know?"

"Hobie, the first thing I want you to know about our daughter is that she's extremely smart and loving. That girl has a heart of gold."

Garth smiled. "Gracie's right. She's quite a girl and would give you her last nickel. She's trusting to a fault."

The sheriff rolled his eyes. "Save all the sweet words in case you need them for a eulogy. I just need the details about why she left."

Gracie's voice cracked. "Eulogy? You don't think she's . . . dead? No, I won't believe it. It's not true. You're a mean, cruel man."

Garth's jaw jutted forward as he grabbed her hand and squeezed. "Of course, it's not true, hon. Hobie, thank you for your time, but we'll be leaving now." He stood and slid out his wife's chair.

"Suit yourself. I have better uses of my time than to be chasing that girl every time she decides to run away."

Garth stood and extended his hand to his wife.

Hobie placed his elbows on the table and buried his face in his hands. "Hold on."

Garth shook his head. "We're getting nowhere. Sorry to have wasted your time."

"I was wrong. I was speaking out of my own pain."

"I'm listening."

"Mary Jane and I lost our seventeen-year-old daughter eight years ago."

Gracie's voice cracked. "I'm sorry. I didn't know. I didn't even realize you'd ever been married."

"I don't suppose anyone in Cartersville knows and that's how I wanted it. I moved here shortly after the divorce. Mary Ann and I were married for eighteen years. Happily. Or so I thought. But after our daughter left home, I discovered our marriage wasn't as solid as I'd wanted to believe. I won't go into why Joanie left, only to say her mother and I each began to blame one another for Joanie's decision. We became brutal in our accusations, and our marriage ended in divorce six months later."

Garth sucked in a lungful of air. "I reckon we've all got our own problems. You ready to go, honey?"

Her sharp glare pierced his heart. "Garth Graham, sit back down."

"But I thought you wanted to go."

"I did when I thought Hobie didn't understand. I was wrong, honey. No one could possibly understand better what we're going through. He'll help us." With a raised brow, she added, "You will help us, won't you, Hobie?"

His chin quivered. "I reckon if Mary Ann and I had confided in a third party who could've helped us face the truth, perhaps we'd still be married. Who knows? But the truth hurt, so we resorted to embrace our own truth, according to what we wanted to believe. Unfortunately, our truths didn't match up and instead of uniting to comfort one another, we fought. I'll do what I can to find your daughter, but I'll need all the information you can give me, even when the truth hurts."

Gracie said, "Everything about her disappearance hurts, but I'll tell all that I think is relevant."

Hobie nodded. "I need to know everything you can tell me about the girl, even if you don't regard it as relevant. Sometimes it's the tiniest, seemingly insignificant details that become the most useful."

"I think I understand. Ludie is smart as a whip. She's a real scrapper."

"So you've said."

Garth nodded in confirmation. Smiling, he said, "What she means is that there aren't many thirteen year old kids could've dealt with all the obstacles she encountered when she ran away the first time. Why, there was the time she had nowhere to go and was sleeping in a bus station, when . . ."

Gracie flinched. "Garth, there's no need in bringing up the past. We need to stick with the present. Besides, I seem to remember it was the train depot, not the bus station."

His lips tightened into a straight line. "Honey, I think I'd know better than you, since I was—"

Hobie said, "Hold it. Do you not see what's happening? The same thing that happened to Mary Ann and me. You start off correcting one another, each claiming to have the real truth. The bickering will become accusations and the accusations will become a sore spot, which will fester and grow into contempt for one another. If that's the way you choose to go with this, then count me out. I can't take it."

Gracie's eyes widened. "I didn't realize that's what I was doing, Hobie, but I'll be more careful to guard my words."

She reached over and with her thumb, lifted her husband's chin. "I'm so sorry, darling. I was wrong. If I had all the answers, we'd know where to look."

When Garth attempted to respond, Hobie thrust out his palm.

"Okay, we're good now. Garth is sorry, you're sorry, we're all sorry. No need to keep rehashing the apologies. Let's get down to business." He picked up a pencil and a tablet. "I think we're ready. Which one is going to tell me what happened to Lucy?"

"Ludie!" Garth corrected. "Her name is Ludie, but I'll let Gracie tell it. She's more of a detailed person and I'm a hit-the-high-spots sort of guy."

Gracie pressed her lips together and closed her eyes. Then, leaning in, she said, "It all began the week I was in bed with phlebitis. The doctor wanted me to stay off my leg. Ludie was a big help. I couldn't have managed without her. At the time we only had four kids staying at the orphanage. Ludie and Mercy made six. Garth had hired a maid to come in and clean, but Ludie did everything for the younger children. It was in the spring, and school was out for the week, since all the farmer's needed their sons to help get the fields ready for planting. It's always a chore making sure the children are all dressed and fed, and lunches are made in time for them to get to class on time, so I was glad it was spring break and less for Ludie to do. It was a Wednesday and Ludie brought me breakfast in bed and told me she planned to take the children on a picnic. I was delighted." She glanced at Garth. "If I'd known then what I know now, I would've insisted that she stay home."

Hobie smiled. "Hindsight is much stronger than foresight. We could all eliminate a lot of heartache if only we could view the future as well as we can analyze the past. So, you're saying the picnic was not a good idea?"

"It was a terrible idea. It was the beginning of troubles. The children came home from the picnic, full of talk about what a wonderful time they had. Ludie had made sandwiches and lemonade, and took them to the creek to swim."

The sheriff said, "Doesn't sound so terrible to me, but I reckon you were thinking it was too much responsibility for the girl to keep an eye on six kids playing in the water. So did you scold her for taking them to the creek?"

"No, it wasn't that. I knew she took them to the shallow end that flows under the bridge. It's where we always take them. It's not deep enough to swim in, but they enjoy wading in the water and chasing minnows."

She paused and looked at Garth. He nodded as if reading her mind, and added, "Besides, Hobie, she wasn't alone. There was someone with her."

"I'm sorry. I must've misunderstood."

Gracie said, "No, you understood correctly. She met a young man while they were there."

"What did she tell you about him?"

"Nothing at that time. When they returned home, the kids were full of talk about what a wonderful time they had. According to what I could piece together from their exuberant little voices, I gathered that before they reached the bridge, they passed a fellow fishing from off the bank, where the river runs into the creek."

"Anyone I know?"

"No, and neither do we. That's the thing. He was a perfect stranger."

Garth rolled his eyes. "I wouldn't use the word perfect, dear, to describe him."

She ignored the comment. "The kids said they asked him if he'd caught anything, and the man held up a nice long string of fish. After he inquired where they were going, they said he grabbed up his tackle box and said he was through fishing and was about to leave when they showed up."

Garth said, "Of course, that was the first lie. What fisherman is gonna leave a spot while he's on a bed? As they left, he followed them. At that point, Ludie should've known he was up to something and should've had sense enough to take the kids home. But, instead, we learned later that she laid out the picnic cloth on the ground and invited a complete stranger to eat with them. I don't know what she was thinking. It wasn't like her. She didn't know the scumbag from Adam. Even if she took no thought for her own safety, she was responsible for the safety of the younger kids."

CHAPTER 16

Gracie nodded in agreement with her husband that Ludie's actions were completely out of character, and had taken them by surprise.

Hobie scratched his head. "Are you two sure you aren't refusing to admit that your little girl has grown into a full-fledged woman at sixteen?" The way he hee-hawed made his statement almost sound vulgar. He jiggled the heavy set of keys attached to his belt. "From what you two have told me about the boy she took up with, I suspect—"

The look on Garth's face was that of a bull dog's. "Hold on. I resent the implication that Ludie—"

When Gracie laid her hand on Garth's forearm, he didn't have to look at her to know it was a plea for him to ignore any perceived implications in order for Hobie to finish his train of thought. Her voice lifted. "What is it you suspect, sheriff?"

"I was about to say that I have a feeling the moment the girl walked up, the fellow lost all interest in fishing for trout. I think he decided to use a different bait and I suspect he caught what he was fishing for."

Garth's face turned red. "And you think that's funny?"

"Perhaps not as funny as it is understandable. I believe you're aware what happens in the Spring . . .the time of year when they say a young man's fancy turns to love. But don't forget that it takes two to tango. Has anyone ever thought to check on when a girl's fancy turns to love? Fall, maybe? Has it occurred to either of you that Lucy might have encouraged him?"

Garth gritted his teeth. "Obviously you aren't keeping up, sheriff. Ludie has never been boy crazy. Never led a boy on. In fact, I'm not sure she's ever even claimed a fellow." He ran his hand over the back of his neck and glanced at Gracie, who sat quietly, twisting a ring on her finger. His tone quickly switched from anger to apologetic. "Well, I don't want to think she'd do such a thing, but to be honest, I don't know what to think anymore. But may I remind you—her name is Ludie."

Hobie shrugged. "That's what I said."

Garth said, "Sorry, Gracie! I'll try to sit quiet and let you finish telling how it all went down."

"It's okay. I know how hard this is for you, sweetheart." Glancing at the ceiling as if attempting to recapture the memory, she murmured, "Let me think. Oh, yes! After the kids got home from fishing that day, I heard them upstairs singing a little ditty, that went something like, 'Ludie and Schooner up in a tree, k-i-s-s-i-n-g. First comes love, then comes marriage, next comes Ludie with a baby carriage."

Gracie could clearly see the sheriff was not taking notes as she'd previously believed, but was merely doodling with his pencil as if he were bored with the whole conversation. When he glanced up, he remarked, "So how did it make you feel?"

"Did you just ask how it made me feel? Suppose you tell me how my feelings will help locate my daughter?"

The sheriff stuck his pencil behind his ear, "Simple. I'm trying to determine if Lucy ran away with the man because she was enamored with him, or if she left home because of your reaction to the situation."

Garth growled. "Her name is not Lucy. Ludie! Ludie! Ludie, Hobart. How many times do we have to tell you? Go ahead and answer, honey. I'm sure when you heard the kids carrying on about Ludie with a baby carriage, it upset you, even though I doubt the little ones understood the implication."

"No, they were having a little innocent fun. Actually, I recall laughing at the silliness, myself. Knowing Ludie's compassionate nature, I wasn't surprised when I learned that she'd offered to share her lunch with the fellow. It would be hard for her to eat in front of someone. She'd always shown good judgment, so when I learned he sat down and ate with them, I didn't think much about it.

But when Ludie came into my room later, I said, "What's this I hear about you having a boyfriend?" I was joking, of course, and expected her to defend herself and say the children were making it all up. So, I was stunned when her eyes lit up and a smile reached from one end of her face to the other. She said, 'Oh, Gracie, I think I'm in love.' *In love?* It was ludicrous. Naturally, I couldn't believe she was serious. But I soon found out that she was not teasing. So, I asked her to tell me all about him, thinking she was infatuated by a good-looking kid she saw fishing. I asked who he was, thinking a new family had moved into the community."

Hobie nodded as if he were one step ahead. He reached for the pencil and put it to the paper. "Try to remember everything Lou-Dee—" he glanced at Garth and grinned while emphasizing the last syllable— "told you about this mysterious stranger."

"Well, she said he was spending the summer with his Grandmother, and . . . "

"Hold on! Who is his grandmother?"

"I asked, but Ludie claimed she didn't know."

"I assume they began seeing one another after that. How did he strike you the first time you met him?"

Gracie swallowed hard. "That's the thing. We've never met him." The admission appeared to open the floodgates to her heart. Unsettling thoughts she'd purposely pushed aside now gushed out with an unstoppable force. Conversations she'd had with Ludie, which she'd closely guarded from Garth, poured out in a conglomeration of emotions. Initially there was fright, then bitterness, anger, but all wrapped up in a blanket of love.

Garth listened as the words spilled out like water pouring over a broken dam. Why had she not told him everything? Did she not trust him?

According to Gracie, Ludie asked two more times that week to go to the creek. Though she had an unsettling feeling in the pit of her stomach, Grace said she didn't want to convey the impression that she didn't trust Ludie, so she relented.

"After school commenced the following week, Ludie began taking long walks alone in the evenings. She's always been an outdoorsy girl, so it was not surprising that she'd want to take time for herself to unwind after a stressful day. . . and what better way to unwind than to take a walk in the woods? Besides, I'd manage to convince myself that I was being overly protective."

The sheriff asked several questions, none of which seemed to be relevant, yet Gracie hoped if she could keep recalling incidents, something would pop up that would lead them to Ludie.

"It was at the supper table one evening about a week later when six-year-old Danny said, 'Schooner made me a fishing pole and let me have some of his worms. I almost caught a fish.'

Garth and I both looked at one another. At first I thought Danny was making it up, but I changed my mind after Garth questioned him."

Garth said, "I don't know when I've been that angry. Ludie had made a lot of mistakes, but even when she'd do something we wouldn't approve of, if we approached her, she wouldn't lie about it. Now, I felt she was not only becoming a liar but she was encouraging the other kids to lie. I couldn't stand for that."

Hobie's brow raised. "I assume Danny is one of the orphans?

Gracie said, "Yes, and he's a cutie, but he's been known to tell a few whoppers. However, when Garth asked about the fellow he called Schooner, Danny looked directly at Ludie and whimpered, 'I didn't mean to tell. I forgot.' Then Ludie jumped up from the table and ran outside. Garth ran after her, and I was left to try to comfort little Danny, who was crying hysterically. He was so upset that he'd broken his promise to Ludie. He's taken a real liking to her, and was afraid she wouldn't have anything to do with him, now that he'd broken his promise."

Garth said, "I was too angry to have a conversation with her. I just ordered her to get back in the house and go to her room, which she did. I had intended to bring it up after I could get control of my emotions, but after mulling it over, I concluded it would be best to let it go. It wasn't as if the boy lived nearby and could become a problem."

Hobie said, "I notice you both switch back and forth referring to him as a boy and a man. Which is he?"

Gracie lifted a shoulder. "That's the thing. Since we've never met him, we can't really say."

"I understand. The evening walks you spoke of—did they cease?"

"No. It never once dawned on me that Ludie was secretly meeting him in the evenings, since I was under the impression he was in Goat Hill for a short visit. Naturally, after weeks passed, I assumed he'd already gone back home."

"And where is home?"

Garth raised a brow. "If only we knew."

"You didn't ask?"

"Never thought it would be important. All I cared about was that his home was not in Goat Hill. As Gracie said, we thought he'd left town and Ludie would get over her school-girl crush and never see him again."

Gracie nodded and said she didn't know they had anything to worry about until one night at the table Mercy remarked that when she got big she wanted a boyfriend like Ludie but she didn't plan to kiss him. "I laughed, then looked at Ludie and jokingly said, 'What makes you think Ludie would kiss a boy?'"

Mercy didn't pause, before saying, 'She kissed Schooner. We saw her when we were playing hide and seek in the woods. Didn't we, Danny?' Daniel lowered his head. That's when I knew this had continued to go on, and Ludie was not only disrespecting us, she was disrespecting the children by her example."

Gracie dabbed at the corner of her eye with a handkerchief. "I looked across the table and seeing the color drain from Ludie's face was proof that Mercy and Danny had both witnessed a shameful display of affection."

Hobie kept his eyes on the paper as he drew circles, inside of circles. "So she kissed a boy . . . and how old did you say she is?"

Garth interjected, declaring age wasn't the issue, that it was Ludie's defiant behavior and blunt refusal to admit wrong-doing after she was caught.

"So, am I to believe you both felt betrayed by the girl's defiant behavior, yet neither tried to meet the boy, to determine if she was in trouble?"

Garth said, "I didn't have to meet the joker to know Ludie was in trouble."

Hobie's eyes widened. "Oh, my, why didn't you say so in the first place?"

"Say what?"

"That she's pregnant."

Garth's mouth gaped open. "I didn't say she was pregnant. I said she's in trouble. I won't have her living under my roof and lying to me."

The sheriff's sideways grin sent chills up Garth's spine.

"Sorry, I suppose I misunderstood, but I keep feeling as if there's something you're holding back. Seems to me if you were truly worried that she was involved in a shameful relationship, you wouldn't have waited so long to look for her." His words seemed cold and hard, as if he were questioning their parenting skills.

Hobie said, "I can see I've offended you, Gracie, and I apologize. Heaven knows, I'm a poor one to criticize, since I failed my own daughter. You've indicated there were things Ludie shared with you that you were afraid to tell Garth. Could we talk about those things?"

"It wasn't that I was *afraid* to tell him. I withheld things for fear of hurting him. Garth and Ludie created a unique bond a few years ago, and I didn't want to share anything that could possibly break that bond. I decided to talk with Ludie in confidence."

"And did you?"

"I did. She insisted that it was love at first sight for them both. According to her, the boy told her he wanted to marry her. Naturally, I tried to make her understand it was puppy love and that she'd be over him—and that he'd be forgotten her by the time he got back home." She acted as if she understood. So, after that I relaxed."

Hobie bit his bottom lip. "I'd say you're very trusting. Maybe you should've locked her in her room."

"What?"

"If I remember correctly, she's quite a looker, and it seems to me you can't stand the thought of the fellows noticing her. The only way to prevent that would be to lock her up. You may have turned away one suitor, but he won't be the last."

Gracie cringed, seeing the sinister smile etch across the sheriff's face. She spoke in a slow, deliberate tone as if conversing with someone who didn't speak her language. In a sense, she wasn't sure he did. "You act as if we should turn our backs when we see an innocent child of ours about to make a big mistake. You'd understand if you had a dau—" She stopped in mid-sentence. "I'm sorry. I forgot."

"Apology accepted. Perhaps I understand more than you realize."

Embarrassed, Gracie plunged ahead in a lengthy monologue. She said Ludie told her the boy had dropped out of school and he worked for his father. "If I remember correctly, she said he was in some sort of retail business. I tried to find out who his folks were, but she said she didn't know. I'm ashamed to say that I had doubts that she was being completely truthful. That hurt, since I'd never had reason to doubt her before. We both cried and out of our anger, we said things neither of us meant. When she clammed up, I stomped out of her room and went to bed. When we awoke the next morning, Ludie was gone."

Gracie looked at Garth and saw the tears making a path down his cheeks. He said, "Hobie if they're off somewhere together, as I suspect, and if he's as wonderful as Ludie seems to think he is . . . then, I hope he'll do the right thing and marry her if—". He paused and bit his lip. "You know what I'm saying. Naturally, we want our daughter back—but more importantly, I want to know that she's safe, happy, and loved the way she deserves to be loved. It's the not-knowing that's driving me crazy."

"That's the right attitude, Garth. The way I see it, the girl is old enough to know what she wants. By your own admission, she left home of her own accord. Now, if we had information to give us reason to believe the fellow forced her to go with him, I promise you, I'd do everything in my power to capture the low-life who kidnapped her. But that isn't what happened, is it Garth? As difficult as it is for you to accept, she made a conscious choice to leave. Since you don't know the boy's folks or where he's from, all we can do is sit tight and wait for them to contact you. I'm sure you'll hear from them soon." Hobie stood, holding out his hand. "Now, if you two will excuse me, I have places I need to be."

Garth's neck stiffened. "That's all the advice you have for us? To wait? That's what we've been doing for months. He jumped up. "Come on Gracie."

On the way home, Gracie burst in to tears. "What good did that do? I wish I'd gone with my first impulse and kept my mouth shut. Nothing was accomplished. I don't think he ever intended to go find her. It's useless, Garth. We'll never see her again. She was so angry the night she left."

Wrapping his arm around her shoulder, he pulled her close. "We aren't giving up, sweetheart."

"Garth . . . Do you think she's . . . living with that ol' boy?"

"I'd bet the buggy on it. But you know Ludie. She's got a good head on her shoulders. She wouldn't take up with just anyone. We have to try to believe that she saw real redeeming qualities in the fellow. I think it was exactly like Ludie told you— love at first sight, and they were too much in love to be separated." He smiled. "You do remember what that feels like, don't you, dear? Remember how your dad did everything he could to keep us apart? Aren't we glad he didn't succeed?"

"Are you saying we should leave them be? Forget about trying to find her?"

"No, but I'm beginning to realize it isn't fair to the other children when we allow vain imaginations to consume our every thought. We have to face facts, sweetheart. We have no leads, but Ludie knows where we are and it's my hope that one day soon, she'll show up at our door with her young man at her side and a ring on her left hand. When that happens, you and i will have a chance to either turn them away or forgive. Which shall it be?"

"You're right. We've wasted precious time dwelling on the negatives, which has only led to anger and frustration. It's time to redirect our thoughts. As difficult as it is to imagine Ludie married, when they do come back, we'll choose to forgive. I'll cook all Ludie's favorite foods and let her know that as much as we wished she'd confided in us, we understand what it's like to be in love."

He chuckled and nodded. "I think we're beginning to understand how the father of the Prodigal Son must've felt. Next, you'll be wanting me to butcher a fatted calf."

"Why not? Nothing is too good for our Ludie." She slid over and snuggled closer. "I only hope she loves him as much as I loved you when Daddy warned me about that awful newspaper guy." She snickered, recalling the memory.

Garth squeezed her hand. "And I hope the ol' boy knows how to love her as she deserves to be loved. I have to believe he does, or lose my mind. Poor girl has been through enough turmoil in her short sixteen years."

She whispered, "What time I am afraid, I will trust in thee."

"I didn't hear you, hon."

"That's okay. I wasn't talking to you."

When he didn't question her further, she knew he understood. Though they were no closer to finding Ludie, Gracie felt a peace flow through her the moment her thoughts were redirected from the frightening vain imaginations to concentrating on good things—things that were true, just and praiseworthy.

Another scripture came to her remembrance—one which might prove harder for her to keep. *"Wait on the Lord; Be of good courage, and he shall strengthen your heart; Wait, I say, on the Lord." Psalms 27:14.* Never considering patience to be one of her virtues, Gracie sighed. Couldn't God give her something a little easier to do?

She closed her eyes and silently prayed: "Lord, if you expect me to sit by and wait, could you please hurry?"

CHAPTER 17

Clemmie and her friend from school, Maurine, became inseparable in the following weeks, studying together, sharing likes, dislikes, exchanging clothes and secrets—yet Clemmie only shared secrets she acquired after becoming born again. To bring up anything that happened before moving in with the Flanigans was not a subject she discussed. All Maurine knew was that she moved to Cartersville from Alabama and that she didn't wish to discuss her past.

The weeks flew by quickly, and posters went up all over school, announcing a Homecoming Dance. Maurine couldn't have been more excited. Clemmie, not so much. Yet, it didn't take long for Maurine to convince her that it would be the most magnificent event she could ever begin to imagine. As she described elaborate decorations, and an out-of-this-world banquet meal, the thought became more appealing.

Although Johnny had been coming around quite often,

Clemmie wasn't ready to court any fellow, and especially not a preacher. Not that she had anything against preachers, but a preacher would certainly have something against her. It was one thing for God to forgive her—or for her to put her past in the past—but it would be deceitful to allow a man of God to marry her. She didn't suppose the Bible said anything about a preacher being able to forget such a vile act as the one she committed. No! She couldn't get involved with a preacher. Not one as nice as Johnny, anyway. If she had to live the remainder of her life an old maid, so be it. She made her bed, so to speak. She bit her bottom lip. The thought of a bed made her stomach turn. If only she could forget, the way God could.

Maurine went home with Clemmie after school, and Carly called the girls into the kitchen for milk and pound cake. When Maurine brought up the school dance, it was difficult to discern who was more excited—Carly or Maurine.

Carly said, "I can't believe you haven't mentioned the dance, Clemmie."

"I'm not going. Johnny doesn't dance."

"Oh!"

Maurine chimed in. "Doesn't matter. Mrs. Flanigan." She's already had two fellows to ask her. She just needs to make up her mind whether she wants to go with Pete or Jesse. They're both divine. I would've simply died if either one would've asked me. I'm going with Andy. He's not the best looking chap, but he's a barrel of laughs, so I know I'll have a good time."

Carly clasped her hands under her chin. "Oh, Clemmie, sweetheart, of course you're going, and you'll be the Belle of the Ball." She quickly added, "You and Maurine, of course. I know both Pete and Jesse and they're from very nice families. You won't go wrong, regardless of which one you choose."

Clemmie didn't want to choose either one, but it would be easier to go to the dance than to try to explain why she'd rather stay home. When Pete called that afternoon to get her answer, she reluctantly accepted.

The night of the dance, Carly spent all afternoon rolling Clemmie's hair and combing it into the latest page-boy style. How lovely she looked.

Clemmie had no doubt the gown Carly picked out was the most expensive in the store, with all the lace and tiny rosettes. But lavender? It was her least favorite color. Did it matter? It wasn't as if she were trying to impress anyone. Especially not Pete Jones. True, he was the best-looking fellow at school—much more handsome than sweet, boring Johnny—yet, he didn't hold a candle against Schooner's handsome looks. She swallowed hard. *Lord. I'm trying to forget. Honest.*

When Pete came to pick her up, Emma couldn't get her eyes off Clemmie, all decked out in her evening clothes. "You look beautiful, Clem. I want to look just like you when I get big and I want Pete to take me to the dance."

Pete grinned and winked. "You got it, kid. I'll be able to say that I escorted the two most beautiful girls in the country to a dance."

Cooper's stoic expression didn't change. Whether it was an indication he didn't find the conversation to his liking, or if he had heartburn was hard for Carly to discern.

After the kids left, she teased him. "Honey, I could see the concern on your face when Pete walked in and looked at your daughter with that look in his eye, as if he'd never seen anything quite as beautiful. She was lovely, wasn't she?"

He turned quickly. "Emma?"

"No, silly. Clemmie."

"Oh. I misunderstood. I thought you said my daughter."

"I did. The night we agreed to make her a part of our family, she became our daughter."

"No, Carly. She didn't. First of all, I never agreed for her to be a part of this family."

"Of course, you did."

"You're wrong. You asked if I thought Emma would like a sister. I thought you were saying you were ready to have another baby. I was thrilled that the depression was lifting, and you were ready to get on with your life."

"I'm sorry, you misunderstood, but regardless, we both got what we wanted. I'm no longer depressed, which was what you wanted, and I got a lovely daughter when Clemmie came into our lives—and that's what I wanted."

"What are you thinking, Carly? Clemmie is a sweet, lovely girl, who came into our lives by divine Providence—but she isn't our daughter. I'd love to have another child, and I hope you're ready, too, but you're becoming obsessed with Clemmie, and that worries me."

"I can't believe what I'm hearing. We didn't give birth to Emma, either, but you never had a problem calling her our daughter. What do you have against Clemmie? Emma loves her like a sister."

He ran his hand over the back of his neck. "Yes, and that worries me. It wasn't Clemmie's idea to stay. You practically forced her into it. Don't you realize Clemmie could decide to go back home at any given time? The longer she stays here, the harder it will be on Emma when she does leave."

"That's ridiculous to say I forced her to stay. It was what she wanted, and she loves it here. Why would she want to go back to an orphanage?"

"Seems I remember you saying that she once told you it was the best thing that ever happened to her."

"That's right, and it broke my heart. That's when I decided that if being sent to an orphanage was the best thing that had happened to her, that her life must've been awful. She deserved to be in a home where people loved her. I know that God sent her to me—to us. Honey, what I've been trying to say is this: I think we should adopt her—make her a real part of our family."

His brow meshed together. "I hope you're joking."

Her jaw flexed. "I'm not, and I'm surprised at your attitude."

Raising his voice, he said, "And I'm surprised at yours. This obsession of yours has taken over our lives. Clemmie is all you think about. You put Emma in bed at night, then go to Clementine's room where I can hear you laughing and talking—sometimes for hours. I'm usually already asleep before you sneak into our bed."

"That's not fair."

"I agree. It isn't fair. You painted her room lavender because you thought it was her favorite color. I have a feeling she hates lavender."

"You're being facetious. It's a beautiful color, and she loves it."

"Did she tell you she loved it?"

"She didn't have to. Any girl would love such a gorgeous room."

"Just as I thought. You fix meals that you think Clemmie likes, you shop for clothes you think she should like. It seems that Emma and I have become after thoughts."

"I'm through having this conversation."

He hung his head. "Me, too. I'm sorry if I upset you. We're both tired and said things we shouldn't have. Let's go to bed."

"You go on. Clemmie will be coming home soon. She'll be excited and want to talk about her night, so I'll wait up for her."

His teeth ground together. "Well, of course you will. What

was I thinking?"

He stormed off toward the bedroom, while she headed to Clemmie's room.

She didn't have long to wait before she heard the front door open. Clemmie opened the door to her bedroom and stopped. "Miz Flanigan. I thought you'd be in bed by now."

"I was waiting up for you, dear."

"For me? Why? Did I do something wrong?"

"Not at all. It's what mother's do, dear. I can hardly wait to hear about your night. I'm sure you had a wonderful time."

"It was okay. But what did you mean by it's what mother's do? You aren't my mother, so there was no need to wait up."

"You're right. I'm not your mother. Not yet, but I don't mind the practice."

Clemmie lifted a brow. "I have no idea what you're talking about, but it's been a long night. Goodnight, Miz Flanigan."

"But don't you want to talk about the dance?"

"Right now, it's the last thing I want to talk about. Goodnight."

Carly reluctantly ambled out and went to bed. She tried to soothe her bruised feelings by reminding herself that she was the mother of a teenager. Weren't they supposed to be moody—not always willing to talk to parents? Shouldn't she be pleased, just knowing her daughter was a normal teen?

Clemmie realized she'd been short with Mrs. Flanigan, but she already had a mother. As fond as she was of Mr. and Mrs. Flanigan, she didn't need another set of parents. Even if she never saw Gracie again, the Graham's were her legal parents , but it was wrong of her to react the way she reacted to someone who had done so much for her. She'd make it up to Mrs. Flanigan tomorrow. But tonight she was sick and tired. Tired of pretending to have a good time, and home sick. Very, very homesick. What she'd give to be at Nine Gables Orphanage among her own people.

The next morning, Cooper walked into the kitchen and saw oatmeal cooking on the stove. For five straight mornings, they had oatmeal. He didn't mind it on occasion, but every single morning? He started out the door.

Carly said, "Where are you going?"

"To work."

"Without eating?"

"Clemmie can have my portion. She loves it. I don't."

Clemmie was standing in the doorway. She smiled. "I was going to offer my serving to you."

He turned around, his gaze locking with hers. "You mean—you don't like it, either?"

She glanced sheepishly toward Carly. "Not really."

Carly said, "But you ate two bowls full when you first came here. I thought you loved it."

"I did. But I was starving. Stone soup would've been good at the time."

"Oh, I am so sorry. Give me five minutes and I'll have you something else to eat. Do you like pancakes?"

Cooper rolled his eyes and left. *She didn't ask me if I wanted pancakes.*

That night, Clemmie lay in bed and could hear the Flanigans' raising their voices. Although she couldn't hear what they were saying, she had a feeling, it had to do with her. Mr. Flanigan had been acting very peculiar, lately. Perhaps it was time for her to think of going home. *Home?* Did she still have a home at Nine Gables? Maybe not, but Grandpa George would take her in. That is, if he was still alive. The horrifying thought that she might never see him again made her sick on her stomach.

CHAPTER 18

The tension between Cooper and Carly increased with every passing day. Cooper pleaded with her to go with him to see a doctor, since he felt she'd begun to live in a make-believe world. But with each blaming the other for the mounting marital problems, Cooper could take it no longer and went to see his good friend, Dr. Nicholas Anders, alone.

The nurse walked into the waiting room. "Mr. Flanigan, the doctor can see you now."

The doctor stood and reached out his hand. "Morning Cooper. What's going on?"

"Nothing with me, Nick. It's Carly."

"Carly? Where is she?"

"She's home."

"Too sick to come? Do I need to make a house call?"

"No. If she knew I was here, she'd be furious. It all started when she brought that girl into our house. Carly and I never had problems until she came to live with us."

"You mean Clementine?

"Yes. You know her?"

"I met her at church. She seems like a sweet girl."

"Well, I suppose she is, but I'm ready for her to find somewhere else to stay."

"What has she done?"

"She's ruining my marriage, that's what."

"It's hard to imagine how such a sweet girl could cause such havoc. Have a seat and tell me what's going on."

Cooper sucked in a heavy breath before beginning. After he finished telling about Carly's bizarre obsession with Clemmie, and how she was beginning to act as if she'd actually given birth to her, the doctor pursed his lips and nodded.

Coop relaxed. It was good to see Nick's reaction and to feel that someone really did understand what he was going through. "Well, that's about it, doc. Now, you understand why I want the girl gone?"

"You're transferring your hostility toward Clementine, when she's not the problem."

"I don't know how you can say that. Carly and I were doing fantastic until she came along."

"Fantastic? Have you forgotten the long talk we had after Carly lost the baby?"

"Well, yeah, but she's over that."

Nick rolled his eyes. "You're wrong. She'll never be 'over that.' She may have moved on to a point that it isn't tormenting her twenty-four-hours a day, but she'll never be over it. She blames herself, and that kind of blame is the most psychological damaging of all. For that reason, you need to be sensitive to her need to express her thoughts if she brings it up."

"I don't know what to say. I seem to always say the wrong thing."

"She doesn't need you to say a thing. She needs you to listen."

"Well, just as she was beginning to act like herself again, there came Clemmie. I need her gone, but I'd feel guilty kicking her out. She's an orphan. How can I get rid of her?"

"Cooper, the problem is not between you and Clementine, but it's between you and Carly."

"I don't agree, but if it is, which one of us is crazy? To be honest, if we don't get help, I'm afraid we're both going to drive the other insane. We always got along so well—until Clemmie showed up." When Nick raised his brow as if to question his statement, Coop shrugged. "Okay, I get what you're saying, and I agree it's not fair to blame her. She didn't ask to stay with us. To be honest, it was almost forced on her. She'd planned to go back to the orphanage, when Carly all but hogtied her, holding her hostage. I know Carly was grateful Clemmie saved Emma. So was I, but must we sacrifice our marriage to show our gratitude?"

Nick sat quietly, allowing Cooper all the time he needed to vent.

"I feel guilty for feeling the way I do. She's a sweet girl and tries hard to please. I know I should be forever grateful to her for saving Emma. And I am, but—"

"Cooper, I understand. You need say no more."

"Do you? I wonder. Because I'm not sure I even understand, myself."

"Have you ever considered how much Clemmie looks like Marly? I have a feeling there's a connection."

He chuckled. "You mean Carly, but I don't see it."

"Actually, I meant Marly, since I think that's who Carly is seeing when she looks at her."

Cooper's face pinched into a frown? Marly? Marly who? I'm not following you."

Now it was the doctor who seemed perplexed. "Her sister."

"Clemmie has a sister? How would you know?"

"Not Clemmie. I'm talking about Carly's sister."

"But she doesn't have a sister."

The doctor flinched. "What?" Scratching his head, he said, "Cooper, I realize you didn't live here when it happened—but are you telling me that Carly has never told you about Marly?"

"Nick, please tell me what you're talking about."

He reared back in the leather swivel chair and rubbed his hand across his mouth as if he didn't know where to begin. "I brought those two into this world and you never saw one without the other. They were the darlings of Cartersville."

Cooper listened intently as the doctor relayed information that he found so shocking, it was hard to take in. According to Nick, Carly and Marly were twins. "When they were fifteen, their parents took them on a boat ride down the river in a new boat. Both girls begged to steer, and Ronnie Dobbs never denied those two anything they asked."

"Who?"

"Their father. From what the authorities could piece together from the grandfather, Tim Dobbs was riding in the boat with them, Marly had the first turn. Then Carly took the wheel, and when she reached back of her to pick up a soft drink, she didn't see the cypress stump and ran the boat smack dab into the center. The boat overturned and Ronnie, his wife and Marly all drowned. Tim, the grandfather grabbed Carly and swam to shore, thinking Ronnie, Freta, and Marly were also swimming behind him. After carrying Carly to safety, Tim went back into the river, searching for them, to no avail. The whole town was in mourning after getting the news."

Cooper couldn't breathe. Why had she never told him? "Where's the grandfather, now?"

"His lungs were never the same after that. He died several months after the accident."

"This is so hard for me to take in. Where did Carly go?"

"She married her high school sweetheart, Julian Dugan. The whole town was relieved that she seemed able to move on with her life, as if nothing happened. But it was a facade. There were deep scars inside that sweet girl that no one could see but me. However, I too, was glad Julian was there for her. She appeared happy, even though those kids didn't have a dime to their name."

"What about the house she was raised in? Didn't she have that?"

"Well, that's still a mystery. It burned to the ground the same week of the accident. The cause of the fire was listed as faulty wiring—and maybe it was."

"I get the feeling you didn't agree?"

He shook his head slowly. "No, but I've never told anyone this but you. I treated Carly after the accident, and she was a mixed-up teenager. She tried to tell me she was Marly and that Carly died."

Cooper's jaw dropped. "Is it . . . was it—"

"True? No. They weren't even identical, although people sometimes had trouble telling them apart when they were little. They both had blond hair and Carly's didn't begin to darken until she was around ten or eleven years old. Marly's stayed much lighter. Marly also had a scar on her left arm, which remained after she pulled a skillet of grease off the stove. Carly had no scar—at least not an outward one. But Carly has carried such a heavy burden of guilt for all these years, and now I think she's convincing herself that Marly has been resurrected through Clementine."

Cooper's jaw jutted forward. "That's just plain stupid. I thought I had problems when I walked in here. Now, I find Carly has lied to me from the beginning of our marriage. What else has she hidden from me, Nick?"

The doctor gnawed on the edge of his bottom lip for several seconds, before responding. "Coop, you came in here blaming Clementine for all your problems. Now, it's all Carly's fault that you're unhappy. Instead of shifting blame from one to the other, why not try to figure out what you can do to help the situation?"

"I'm not the one who lied."

Nick stood. "Well, good luck with that attitude."

He groaned. "I'm sorry. This has all been such a shock, I can't think straight. Tell me what to do, doc. I want to save my marriage."

CHAPTER 19

Clemmie eased the front door shut, pulled off her heels and tiptoed down the hall to her room. Stunned to see Mrs. Flanigan sitting on her bed, she bit her lip to keep from saying something she might regret.

"You're home early, dear? Are you not feeling well?"

"I feel fine, but Miz Flanigan, but I've told you there's no need to wait up."

"Fiddlesticks. I do it because I want to, sweetheart. But hearing you call me Mrs. Flanigan makes me feel as if we're hardly acquainted. Aunt Carly might be nice. What do you think?"

She flinched. "I reckon I'll have to think on that, Miz Flanigan." Clemmie thought it strange when the woman acted almost pleased that her suggestion didn't meet with approval.

"Oh, sweetheart, I understand. I do! It wasn't my first choice, either. Actually, I've grown to love you like a daughter, but I was afraid you might not be comfortable referring to me as 'Mama, although I would certainly have no objections. You seem more like a daughter to me than a niece." She threw up her hands. "Look at me, trying to influence your decision. You should choose whatever seems more appropriate to you." Then patting the mattress, she said, "We can decide on that later. Sit down and tell me all about your exciting evening. Johnny is such a sweet fellow, I think it's wonderful that you two are so compatible. I couldn't be happier for you both."

Clemmie gave a slight chuckle as she pounced down on the edge of the bed. "Exciting? Our outings are about as exciting as watching water drip from a pump."

Carly giggled. "I don't understand."

"Well, I reckon if you're real thirsty and the well's dry, a drip is better than nothing."

"Oh, I think I get it now. Who needs an ocean to quench a thirst, if all one needs is within reach. I agree. I'm sure you have plenty of fellows vying for your attention, but when the right one comes along, you need no other suitors. You're a very sensible young lady. I suppose Johnny took you to a picture show? There isn't much else to do in this little town."

"Unfortunately, Johnny feels it would be inappropriate for a minister to be seen at a theatre. So, we rode over to the Snack Shop for a malted milk and a hotdog, then sat in the car and watched the people going into the diner."

"How nice. It gave you two time to be alone without distractions. He's rather quiet when he's around us, but I suppose you two find plenty to talk about when you're together. Am I right?"

"Not really. There are quite a few awkward moments when neither of us can think of anything to say. He turned on the radio and we sat there and listened to his choice of music until I got sleepy and asked him to bring me back. Frankly, I think he was glad I suggested it."

"I think that's perfectly normal."

"Really? Did you have trouble thinking of something to say when you and Mr. Flanigan first met?"

Carly was slow to answer. "No because I was in love with my husband, and Cooper meant nothing more to me than a way to get us where we needed to go."

"But surely you couldn't help notice how good-looking he is."

"If I did, I don't remember. Julian was so depressed, all I cared about at the time was trying to help him. Cooper and I became friends out of necessity, but the friendship grew, and eventually we realized we had fallen in love. I'm happy that you and Johnny are getting along so well. You're very sweet, and he has such a mellow personality."

Clemmie grinned. "I think it might be more interesting if he weren't so mellow. I'd prefer green or rotten. I find mellow to be rather dull."

"You're being funny, but you'll feel differently after y'all get better acquainted, which will happen as you continue seeing one another. You *would* like to know him better, wouldn't you? He's such a nice, polite young man. A girl sure wouldn't go wrong marrying a fine Christian man like Pastor Johnny."

"Marry?" Her lip quivered. "I'm never getting married. Never!"

"Oh, honey, don't say that. Sure, you will. God loves you very much and he has already picked out someone for you."

Her jaw dropped. You don't reckon it's Johnny, do you?"

"Don't you worry, dear. If Johnny is not the one the Lord has chosen for you, trust God to reveal it to you in His time."

She blew out a long breath of air. "I got a feeling I'm hearing from God, already."

"I have no doubt." Clementine Graham was a hard one to figure, but it was understandable. From all indications, the teen had been through a lot of trauma in her short lifetime. It would take patience and lots of understanding to win her confidence.

"Miz Flanigan, there's something about me that you don't know." She shrugged. "Actually, there's a lot about me that you don't know, but I reckon you're better off not knowing everything." Clemmie noticed her wince at being referred to as Miz Flanigan, but it was the only thing that felt natural. "I'm sorry . . . I hope you aren't offended."

"Offended? Not at all. I'm sure something will come to you in time, and you'll come up with your own affectionate term, that feels right for you."

"You're mighty kind, Miz Flanigan . . .." She paused and smiled. "I get it, now!"

"I beg your pardon?"

"I'm beginning to understand what you meant when you said Miz Flanigan sounds kinda formal, but Aunt Carly just doesn't roll off my tongue, natural like. You're Miz Flanigan to Maurine, but you're more than that to me."

Carly's lip trembled. It was what she'd been waiting to hear. "Really, dear?"

"Yes'm, it just came to me and the more I dwell on it, the better I like it."

"Oh, honey, I think I'm gonna cry. Say it, sweetheart!"

"Miz Carly!" She repeated it. "Miz Carly. Yes'm, that's it. Right personal sounding, don't you think?

It was an improvement, but not what Carly was hoping for. However, she couldn't deny a little progress was better than none.

CHAPTER 20

Though it was what Carly had prayed for, she was taken aback the night she and Clemmie were washing dishes and seemingly out of the blue, Clemmie made a surprise announcement.

"Miz Carly, you've asked me who my folks are, and at first I thought you were just being curious. But you've shown me you really do care about me." She paused as if second-guessing her decision to continue. "So, I've been thinking I ought to tell you my story, the way Uncle George told it to me." Her face lit up. "Everybody called him Uncle George, so I did too. That is, until I learned who he really is."

"And who is he?"

"My grandpa."

"I had a grandfather. We called him Paw Paw. Grandfathers are wonderful, aren't they?" Carly hung up her drying cloth and said, "Come on. Let's let the dishes dry themselves. We'll go to your room, where I'd like to hear everything there is to know about your grandfather."

"Everything?" Clemmie hung her head. "Gracious me, I think I may have said too much already, but I don't 'spect there's no backing up now."

"Too far? Honey, you haven't said anything."

"You might change your mind about me when you hear the whole truth. Miz Carly, back where I come from there was a rich family by the name of Gladstone. Mr. Gid was the old man, and he had two daughters. One named Alamanda and the other one was Delia."

Carly's eyes lit up. "Wait a minute. I know those names. There was a family of Gladstones in Goat Hill, Alabama near Marl where Cooper and I lived before moving to Cartersville."

"Yes'm, I know where Marl is, and that would be the same bunch."

"But what's the connection with you?"

"Mr. Gideon P. Gladstone was my great-grandpappy."

"Your . . . *grandfather?*"

"Great-grandfather. Yes'm, although I ain't bragging since I ain't real proud of it."

"But how—"

"How did I wind up scrounging off good folks like you and Mr. Cooper?"

"That's not what I meant to imply." She shrugged. "I don't consider you scrounging off us, since we invited you here. But I do wonder how a Gladstone descendent could've wound up in

Cartersville with nothing but the clothes on your back. Please continue."

"Don't say I didn't warn you, and if you want me to leave after you hear the truth, I won't hold it against you."

Cooper stuck his head in the door. If he tried to hide his shock when he saw his wife and the little swamp urchin acting as if they were having a slumber party, he failed. "Hon, it's getting awfully late. Aren't you coming to bed?"

"I'll be in shortly, dear. Don't wait up."

After he closed the door, Carly said, "Now, pick up where you left off."

"Well, I promised my grandpa I'd never tell, and I reckon I oughta be ashamed for breaking my word. But I feel I owe it to you since you've been so kind and it's the only thing you've asked from me. Delia Gladstone was my grandma, although she died before I was born, so I never had the pleasure of meeting her."

Carly didn't know whether the girl had made up the fib years ago or if she'd been told the outlandish story by the old man and believed it to be true. "Dear, although I'll admit I never personally met the Gladstone family, they are well-known in South Alabama. My former neighbor knew them well, and she shared with me the sad story of Delia's death. According to what I was told, the beautiful young girl went off to a finishing school, and it was there that she became ill with the flu and died. I understand her mother grieved herself to death over the loss of her beautiful daughter. Honey, perhaps your grandmother was also named Delia and you could've possibly heard stories passed down and confused the two names. But Delia Gladstone never had a child. The poor girl died at a young age, before she had a chance to marry."

"That's what folks was told, ma'am, but it weren't the truth. The truth is, my grandma didn't die of the flu and she didn't go off to no finishing school. She was secretly dashed away to New Orleans because she was pregnant with my mama, who they named Comfort. That's a real pretty name, don't you think?"

Carly nodded. "Lovely, indeed."

"Grandma Delia upped and died not long after Mama was born, and the Gladstones never found out that Grandpa George was the baby's father. And they had no idea that Cleo, who was George's sister and worked on the Gladstone Plantation, was raising their own flesh and blood in a little shanty within hollering distance of the mansion."

"Oh, m'goodness, child, who told you such an outlandish story?"

"But it's true. My grandpa George told me and he oughta know, since he was the baby's daddy."

Carly tried to hide her shock. "Your grandfather . . . so it's true? Old man Gideon was your great-grandfather?" She quickly added, "Not that I thought you were making it up, but I did wonder if you were possibly confusing your grandmother's name with the Gladstone girl's.

"No'm. Nothing confusing about it. I've only told one other person."

"Well, I feel honored that you entrusted me with your secret. I think I understand. Delia's family carefully shielded the truth because their daughter was unwed, which would've been scandalous if it had become public."

"Oh, no'm. That ain't the way it happened. She was married, alright, but Grandma Delia's folks didn't know. My Grandpa George's pappy married them before my mama was born."

"Very interesting. So where's your mother, now?"

"Don't reckon nobody knows. Grandpa said Comfort's downfall was her beauty. I was told that by the time the boys began to notice her—if you know what I mean--she ran off and started dancing in juke joints, passing."

Carly's eyes widened. "You've lost me. I thought we were talking about your grandfather and Delia Gladstone's illegitimate child."

"Yes'm." She paused and chewed the inside of her cheek. "If that word–illegitimate—means 'not real,' then it don't apply, because my mama was real, all right."

"Of course, she was. I agree it isn't a very good word to describe a child born out of wedlock. Please finish."

"Wedlock? That's a peculiar word, ain't it? But like I said, they were married, for sure. My grandpa said they were married in the sight of God. Ain't that a fine thought to know God was right there watching them? According to Grandpa George, Grandma Delia was the prettiest woman he ever laid eyes on. Says she had hair like cornsilk and eyes like emeralds. According to him, my mama looked just like her, cornsilk hair and all. Said I got eyes just like them. I wonder what I'd look like with cornsilk hair."

"Your hair is beautiful, but I'm still confused. I don't understand what you meant by saying she was passing."

"It ain't so hard to figure out. Don't you see? Comfort favored her mama, Delia Gladstone."

Carly attempted to hide her shock. "You aren't saying that . . . are you trying to say your Grandfather George was—?"

"Colored? Yes'm." She smiled big and threw her shoulders back. "And the same blood that runs through his veins runs through mine. I was thirteen before I learned that the sweet old caretaker that everybody called Uncle George was really my grandfather. But I ain't lying when I say nothin' ever made me as proud as I was the day I learned I b'longed to somebody and that somebody was ol' George."

"But you look—" Carly seemed to have trouble finishing her sentences.

Recalling something Grandpa warned her about, it was if a tardy bell went off in her head. She quickly slid her feet off the bed, stood and walked over to the back door. "You've been most kind and I sure appreciate the food, Miz Carly, but I reckon it's time for me to be on my way."

"Where do you think you're going?"

"If it's agreeable with you, I'll camp out by the river tonight, but I promise to look for another camping spot tomorrow."

Carly stood and plumped the pillow on the cot. "What are you talking about? You'll do no such thing. But it's late and we both should get to sleep. I didn't mean to keep you up so long I hope you sleep well."

Clemmie smiled. "Thank you, Miz Carly."

After Carly went to bed, Clemmie lay awake pondering. Why was the woman so good to her? Was it because she found out she was a Gladstone, and it didn't matter that she was colored—or was it that she was colored and it didn't matter that she was a Gladstone? The amusing thought made her smile.

CHAPTER 21

Garth and Gracie had put the children to bed, and breathed a heavy sigh of relief. It had been a trying day. The lady from the Welfare Department had brought them a very disturbed little girl that morning. Olene, who insisted she be called Swifty, threw a tantrum at lunch and insisted she was going on a hunger-strike and didn't intend to eat until she was reunited with her mother. Twice, within a three-hour period, she attempted to run away.

Garth looked up from his newspaper at his exhausted wife and with a wink, said, "If Swifty tries it again, I suggest we not go looking for her. She's a tough little bird."

Gracie tried to pretend it wasn't funny, though it was difficult to keep from laughing. "Shame on you, Garth Graham. But does she remind you of someone?"

"Yep! Two peas in a pod. I didn't think there was another Ludie in the world, but I'm beginning to see I was wrong."

When someone knocked at the door, Gracie jumped up and

grabbed the newspapers Garth had thrown on the floor. "Good grief, who could that be? I've spent the entire day trying to get Olene settled and this house is a disaster. Quick, take the coffee cups to the kitchen and I'll answer the door."

A tall, handsome young man stood, holding his hat in his hand. "Good evening, ma'am. Forgive me for calling so late, but I've just got into town. I suppose I should've waited until morning, but to tell the truth, I felt I couldn't wait any longer."

Garth stepped up to the door at the sound of a strange, male voice and flipped on the porch light. "Can I help you?"

The young man shuffled on his feet, and stuttered. "'Evening sir. I wondered if . . . I have no right to ask, but—I don't know how to begin. But, I need—"

"I'll tell you what you need. You need to slow down and breathe. Then we'll discuss why you showed up at my door at this time of night."

When Gracie gave Garth the "look," he realized he sounded like an ogre. Feigning a smile, he reached out his hand. "Graham here. And you?"

"Uh . . . me? Alexander, sir."

"Well, now that we have that out of the way, what can I do for you?"

Beads of sweat on his upper lip glistened under the light. "I apologize for waiting so late to come—"

Garth felt the ire rising. "I believe we've covered that. Now, if you don't mind, please say what you came to say. I've had a very long day." He felt Gracie pulling on his shirttail, her silent way of saying, "Be nice." But how long did she expect him to stand there with the door open, letting the cold air blow in?

As if she were reading Garth's mind, she reached for the young man's hand and said, "For goodness sake, there's no need in us all standing here in the cold. "Won't you come in?"

Garth blinked. "Hon, if you're cold, why don't you go on inside and I'll step out on the porch with Alexander until he decides he's ready to tell me what he's doing here."

Her eyes squinted, and speaking through clenched teeth, she said, "That's not necessary. We'll all go inside. Won't you come in, Alex? You don't mind if I call you, Alex, do you?"

"No ma'am, but Alexander is my—" He shrugged. "No ma'am. That's just fine."

Garth rolled his eyes and feigned a yawn, although Gracie pretended not to notice. She ushered the stranger into the parlor. He said, "Now that we're all warm and toasty, suppose you tell us what we can do for you. Do you need money? Food? Gas? We can't help you if we don't know what you want."

The stranger took a seat and licked his lips. "I understand, sir. I'm a friend of Ludie's, and I was wondering if I might speak with her. I've tried to get up the nerve to come, all day, but I knew I wouldn't be able to sleep tonight, if I didn't come."

Garth and Gracie glared at him. Her heart pounded. Alex was such a clean-cut, polite fellow—the kind of boy she'd hoped Ludie would show an interest in.

He must've noticed the shock on their faces, because he eased to the edge of his seat, while wringing his hands. "She told you, didn't she? What I did to her was unforgiveable. I know how much she loved me. I only wish it hadn't taken me so long to realize how much I loved her. Could you please tell her I have to see her? And if I may be so bold, would you mind if I speak to her privately?"

Gracie glanced at her husband. Ludie was quite popular at school and had plenty of young men vying for her attention, but Gracie couldn't recall Ludie mentioning anyone by the name of Alexander. Yet, this young man appeared to be everything they'd prayed for, for their daughter. He was every girl's dreamboat.

Her gaze locked with her husband's. It was evident Garth was thinking the same thing she was thinking. Should they tell him? Not everything of course. But if Alex and Ludie were as close as he indicated, perhaps Ludie said something to him before she left—something that might lead them to her. It was beginning to make sense why she would've run off. She was obviously heartbroken and was on the rebound. It was just like her to run away with the first creep to come along. Ludie had a history of reacting to unpleasant situations before taking time to think things through, rationally.

Garth looked at his wife. "Should I?"

She nodded.

He cleared his throat. "Alexander, I hope you won't think less of our daughter when I tell you what I'm about to say."

"Sir, nothing could make me think less of Ludie. There'll

never be another girl for me. I just pray she'll forgive me."

"Excuse us, please, Alex. I'd like to speak to my husband in the next room. Please don't think us rude."

"No ma'am. I'd never think that. But, would you please tell Ludie come out to the porch? I'll be waiting."

Garth said, "Honey, I know what you're thinking, and the answer is yes. "It's obvious he cares a lot for Ludie, and I think it's only fair that we tell him the truth. The whole truth—or at least as much of it as we know."

The young man's eyes widened. "She's alright, isn't she? Please . . . can I see her?"

"Son, I only wish I could go upstairs and call her to come down. But she's not here."

"Where is she? When will she be home?"

"We wish we knew. She ran away with some no-good drifter and we—"

Gracie gave her husband the eye, which he understood to mean he was saying too much. She said, "What Mr. Graham means is that Ludie was going through a traumatic time—and now that we've met you, I think I understand why she needed to get away."

He lowered his head. "I'm sorry about that, ma'am. I was a jerk."

"No! No, you misunderstood. I wasn't blaming you. I only meant that Ludie was suffering from rejection. I don't know how much she shared with you, but she was an orphan when she came here, so she'd already dealt with feelings of separation anxiety. It's clear to me now, that when you didn't appear to share her romantic feelings, the added rejection was too much for her. Heartbroken, she left with the first fellow who came along. He was merely her way out of here. But that isn't your fault."

Gracie was touched when she saw moisture welling in his eyes. Poor kid . . . it was obvious he really loved their Ludie, and he was everything she could ever hope for, for Ludie. It took real guts for him to come there and pour out his heart. If only there was a way to let Ludie know how much he really cared. Garth felt she might've married that rascal she left with, but after meeting Alex, it was easy to understand why her heart was broken and that she only used the other fellow to get out of town. But where did she go?

Alex appeared unable to take in what he was hearing. "So, you're saying after she left with . . . whoever she left with . . . that she's never come back?"

Garth nodded. "That's right."

With his elbows planted on his knees, Alex buried his face in his hands. "Oh, Ludie what have I done?"

Gracie walked over and sat beside him on the sofa. "Don't take it so hard, son. We don't blame you. Ludie has always had trouble facing adversity. This isn't the first time she's run away. She came back the last time, and I'm sure she'll come back this time, yet I can't help worrying about her."

Alexander stood. "I'll find her, ma'am. I promise. I won't stop looking until I find her. I just assumed that she came home after she—well, I thought she'd be here."

"Thank you for not giving up on her. Ludie has trust issues, but I always said when the day came that she'd fall in love, she'd fall with her whole heart. I now understand that's exactly what happened."

"I'm sorry to have stayed so late. I'll be going now, but if you hear from her, would you please notify me?"

He shook hands with Garth, but Gracie wrapped him in a hug. "I'm so glad you came. It's good to know she has someone else who loves her as much as we do."

Just as he was walking to his car, Gracie went running after him. "Wait!"

"Yes ma'am?"

"Supper will be served at seven o'clock tomorrow night. We'd love it if you'd come eat with us."

"That's mighty kind of you ma'am. But are you sure? You don't really know me, and you might not be so hospitable if you did."

She dismissed his remark with a wave of her hand. "Fiddlesticks. I hope to know you better, but for now, I know all I need to know. We usually eat a little earlier, but Garth has a business meeting tomorrow at 5:30, and probably will be late getting home. We'll be expecting you."

"Thank you, ma'am. Then, I'll be here at seven."

After he drove away, Gracie said, "Oh, Garth, what a nice young man. Such a gentleman. It's easy to see that he's been raised right."

"I agree, he certainly made a good impression. I'm convinced he wants to find Ludie as much as we do. He's the kind of fellow I hoped Ludie would take up with, but she always seemed to be drawn to the bad boys who chose to spend their time loafing. This one has a good job and a head on his shoulders. Are you sure she never mentioned him to you?"

"I'm sure. But I suppose she was too humiliated, after she expressed her feelings to him and he didn't reciprocate."

The clock in the foyer struck ten times. Garth said, "I'll never understand women, and I sure won't be able to figure out the most complicated one of all, tonight. Let's go to bed. Tomorrow will come early."

Gracie had never felt as energetic as she did the following day. Though she'd tried to conjure up hope that she'd find Ludie, it was difficult to keep believing until Alexander showed up at their door. Was God trying to tell her to keep the faith?

The house was spotless, the ham was cooked, potato salad made, peas hot on the stove, and the pecan pie was still in the oven. She paced the floor, waiting for her guest.

At precisely seven o'clock, Alex rang the doorbell. Garth followed his wife's instructions and had him sit in the parlor to give them time to become better acquainted, while she made the sweet iced tea. Most folks in Goat Hill only drank iced tea in the summer, even though the thermometer hadn't yet dipped below

205

forty, but Garth drank it year-round. She hoped Alexander would like it.

What an amazing young man—so very gracious and he couldn't stop bragging on the delicious meal. Gracie had waited all evening to bring up the subject that was utmost on her mind and she hoped it was on his, also.

"Alexander, we didn't really have a chance to talk last night. I'm glad you accepted our invitation. I have a few questions."

"I'm sure you do, ma'am. I'm truly sorry for hurting her. I've never known a girl like Ludie, and well . . . I reckon I didn't know how to treat her right. That's no excuse, I know, but I've tried to figure me out and I've concluded I'm just plain stupid."

"I'm sure you're being much too hard on yourself. I can tell you're older than our Ludie, so I don't suppose you met her at school."

"No ma'am. I finished school four years ago." His eyes widened. "I hope that isn't a problem."

"Of course not. There's several years difference in mine and my husband's age."

"I met her at a picnic, and I thought she was the prettiest girl I'd ever seen. She made my heart beat faster every time I looked at her. I'd courted pretty girls before, but not one has ever had that effect on me."

Garth rolled his eyes. "Did you do something that caused her to run away?"

He lowered his head. "Yessir, I reckon I did. No need to lie, but if I could just have one more chance, I promise you, I'd never do anything to hurt her again. Never!"

Gracie glanced at her husband sharply. "We believe you. Don't we, dear?"

Garth gave a reluctant nod.

Alexander stood, and reached out his hand. "Thank you ma'am for a delicious meal. You sure are a good cook. And sir, I meant what I said. If I ever get another chance, I promise to take real good care of your daughter." He started out the door, then turned as if he'd had an afterthought. "I have no right to ask favors, but if you could grant me just one, I'd appreciate it if you wouldn't mention me if she gets in touch with you."

"But why? I'd think you'd want her to know how much you care."

"No ma'am. I'm afraid if she hears I'm looking for her, she'll say she doesn't want to see me, and that would put you in an awkward position. You'd be obligated to abide by your daughter's wishes. Understand? If she makes up her mind not to see me, I'll never get to tell her how I feel. I simply must have an opportunity to talk with her face-to-face before that happens."

Garth shook his hand and said, "I hear what you're saying. You have our word, we'll let you two work it out in your own time, won't we sweetheart?"

"If you really think it best."

"I do, ma'am. Thank you folks. I'll keep in touch. After meeting you, I'm even more convinced that she'll come back here.

I just wish I knew where she is now."

After he left, Gracie said, "Oh dear. How will we notify him if Ludie does come home? We don't have an address or his phone number."

"If he's as crazy about her as he says, we won't have to wait long for him to get in touch with us. But Gracie, I'm afraid you and Alex are both getting your hopes up, only to have a big letdown. You're only fooling yourself if you think she's not already married. Think about it. Don't you know in your heart that she would've been home by now if she wasn't married? The best thing we can do for her is to hope she's happy."

"Garth Graham, if hoping could change things, I'd be hoping she's not married. Then we'd all be happy."

CHAPTER 22

Carly Flanigan hardly slept a wink, thinking about Clementine's background. She loved the girl before, but having her share her family secret made her feel even closer to her.

How blessed she was the day God placed Clemmie in their lives. Not only had she saved Emma, in a way she saved the whole family. She had to let her go, though, if that's what she really wanted. Perhaps Emma was right and she really was a Swamp Angel and had done what the Lord had sent to do. It was all Carly could think about all morning.

That afternoon she was sweeping the front yard, when Clemmie and Emma came walking home from school, holding hands. Her throat tightened as she watched the beautiful, willowy figure swinging Emma by the hand. They were both giggling. What was it about Clemmie that reminded her of Marly? Though she and Marly were twins, they were as different as cats and dogs when it came to their personalities. Carly had always been very conservative with her money, her words, and her ability to make friends. Marly, on the other hand was spontaneous, funny, and popular. She said what she thought, yet was never offensive—she was the twin that Carly had always wanted to be.

But was Cooper right? Was Clemmie really happy living there, or had Carly unwittingly made it difficult for her to leave? When Coop first told her about his consultation with Dr. Nick, Carly was furious. But after mulling his words over, she couldn't deny there was truth in what he said. Clemmie had brought up going back to the orphanage more than once, but Carly wouldn't hear of it. It was not until after talking with Dr. Nick that she began to understand what she'd unconsciously been doing. He asked a very poignant question that set her teeth on edge and made her want to lash back at him—until she realized he was right in asking it. He said, "Tell me, Carly, are you trying to hold on to Clemmie because you feel she needs you—or is it because you need her?"

She knew the answer, though she wasn't proud. As much as she hoped Clemmie would not bring up leaving again, she wouldn't attempt to stop her if she did. After several sessions with Dr. Nick, she began to understand that although she was driving the boat when it overturned, that it was an accident. But it was when he asked her if her mother, father, sister and grandfather could come back for a day, to imagine what they might say to her. Would they be angry and blame her for their deaths? Or would they hug her and tell her it wasn't her fault, and that they loved her after death as much as they did in life?

It was after imagining such a reunion that the guilt seemed to slither off her heavy shoulders. She could picture them . . . hugging, laughing, the way she remembered them.

After that, the relationship between her and her husband greatly improved in days to follow. The fighting ended and she found herself falling in love with Coop all over again with the same passions she felt when they first married. He'd begun to look at her with the same spark in his eyes that he had when they first fell in love. Life was good again.

The girls went inside and Carly moaned, seeing Pearl Greene's car coming down the road. She stuck her head in the door, and yelled, "Clemmie, I fear I'm about to have company but I'll entertain her on the porch. Please get you and Emma a piece of Caramel Cake from the pie safe and pour you both a glass of milk."

"Thanks, I will. After I help Emma get into her play clothes I'll be in my room studying for tomorrow's exam, if you should need me."

"That's fine, dear. I'm hoping the visit will be a short one."

Pearl pulled into the yard, and yelled, "Hello, Carly. You look like you could do with some company."

"Sure, Pearl. Come on up and have a seat. It's such a lovely day, we'll sit outside."

"I saw your car parked in the yard. Coop must've taken off early. I suppose he's inside?"

Carly winced. So that's why she stopped. "I'm sorry, Pearl, he isn't here. Coop rode to work with one of the laborers and left the car for me. I had some running around to do."

"Oh!" The disappointment on her face was quite evident. "Well, I didn't intend to stay long, but I thought I'd drop by and see if everything was okay."

"Okay? Why wouldn't it be?"

"No reason. None, that is, unless that girl is still hanging out here."

Carly ignored the remark. "Don't you love the cool weather we've been having recently?"

"Yes, it's nice." Her eyes squinted into little slits. She glanced toward the door, then leaned in toward Carly and whispered. "Well, is she?"

"To whom are you referring, Pearl, and is she what?"

"That Clementine girl. I want to know if she's still here."

"Why?"

"For goodness sake, Carly. I love you and Coop and I worry about you both. As your best friend, it stands to reason that I'd be curious as to how things are working out with the girl."

"Thank you for your interest. Clemmie is doing fine but it's sweet of you to be so concerned."

"So she is still here. I was afraid of that. Law, Carly, you're inviting trouble. I know Coop loves you, but honey, he's a very handsome man and she has the looks men go for. It isn't fair to Cooper to let her continue to hang out here. Men will be men, and to allow such temptation to be waltzing around in front of your husband, night after night is inviting trouble."

"I see your point, Pearl."

"You do?"

"Sure. I'll have a talk with her about her waltzing."

"Carly Dugan, you beat all. Well, you can poke fun all you want but mark my word, she's staying here for a reason and I know what it is." She glanced at her watch. "What time do you expect Cooper to get home?"

"He'll probably be very late since he's riding with one of his men. He won't get home until after they get everything cleaned up."

"That's too bad." She stood and picked up her pocketbook. "Well, I've enjoyed the visit, but I suppose I should be getting back to the house."

Carly walked her to her car, then breathed easier as she watched her drive away. No woman could get her goat the way Pearl Greene could.

****

Clementine awoke Saturday morning to the smell of sausage frying. She hurried out of bed, dressed and walked into the kitchen.

Carly said, "Good morning, Sunshine. I trust you slept well."

"I was very comfortable . . .but I can't say that I slept well. Ma'am, as much as I appreciate the warm hospitality, I've decided to go back to Alabama."

"To the orphanage?"

"No'm. I plan to stay in Grandpa's log shanty, back of the orphanage, even though he won't be there."

"I'm sorry, dear. Passed away?"

Clemmie's eyes widened. The possibility hadn't crossed her mind. "Goodness gracious, I hope not. He moved into the basement of the orphanage a few years ago. The shanty is empty, now and although it has its downsides, I made some wonderful memories in that little one-room shack. It'll suit me fine to live there."

"We'll miss you. I only hope you're making the right decision."

"And I thank you, ma'am. Grandpa's old and I got no right to keep burdening him with worry. After all, he's my blood kin. I gotta go back and let him know I'm okay." Reaching into her pocket, Clemmie pulled out a tiny trinket box and held it out for Carly to see. "I ain't got no money, and all I got is this ring. I know it ain't worth much, but maybe it's worth the price of a bus ticket to Grandpa's. I plan to sell it. I don't reckon you'd be interested?"

When Carly didn't immediately respond, Clemmie closed the box and dropped it back in her pocket. "I didn't think so."

"Hold on, dear. It's a wedding ring, isn't it? Was it Delia's ring? I suppose your grandfather gave it to you. I'll buy you a bus ticket, but I won't take the ring. I'm sure it has a lot of sentimental value."

"Nah, it didn't belong to nobody special, but I promise it's mine. I didn't steal it."

Carly wiped the flour from her hands onto her apron,. "Well, of course you didn't. That never crossed my mind. She walked over to the pie safe and reached for a large cookie jar, sitting on top. Reaching in, she pulled out five one-dollar bills, and handed them to Clemmie.

"No ma'am. Can't take it. I ain't asking for no charity. Just need to sell the ring for enough money to get me a ticket."

Since the girl seemed determined to conceal the whereabouts of the orphanage, out of respect for her wishes, Carly dared not ask, though she assumed it was nearby . . . perhaps Atlanta. "May I look at the ring once more?"

Clementine pulled out the box and opened it.

Carly took the ring and holding it between her thumb and ring finger, she held it up to the light to examine. "Oh my goodness."

"What's wrong?"

"Sugar, after viewing it in the light, I realize this is not junk. It's a beautiful piece of jewelry, and worth much more to me than the five dollars I offered. If you'll take ten bucks, then we'll both feel as if we've made an excellent deal."

"Ten dollars? You must be jiving me. Them little diamonds ain't real. I don't figure it's worth more'n half-a-dollar, if that much. It's just a piece of junk."

"Clemmie, one person's junk can be another person's treasure. If you'll accept my offer, I will treasure the ring forever. Embracing her in a spontaneous hug, Carly said, "Emma will be so disappointed when she learns you've gone home, but I'm sure you're doing the right thing. I don't know what you've been running from, dear, but I'll be praying for all things to work together for your good."

"That would be a mighty tall order, even for God, I reckon."

"Honey, don't you know there's nothing impossible with God? Whatever concerns you, concerns him. After breakfast, Cooper can drive you to the bus terminal."

"It ain't so far to town, and I think the walk will do me good. It'll give me time to think. If it's alright with you, though, I'll wrap up a sausage biscuit and take with me on the bus."

"Take a couple with you and get you two or three apple tarts from the pie safe. I don't know how far you're traveling, but you'll need lunch when you arrive at your destination. I'll pour some lemonade in a Mason jar to wet your whistle."

"Thank you, ma'am. I don't know why you're so good to me, but I'll forever be grateful for your kindness. Please kiss little Emma for me and tell her I won't never forget her."

Carly watched out the window until Clemmie was out of sight.

Cooper sneaked up behind his wife and wrapped his arms around her waist. He kissed her on the side of her face, then wiped her cheek with the back of his hand. "Hey, what's with the tears?"

"She's gone, Coop. This time for good."

CHAPTER 23

Eliza Clementine Graham sat with the side of her face resting on the cool window, observing the sights along the way, as the bus headed toward Goat Hill, Alabama. The hardwoods were losing their leaves and the pecan trees were loaded down with pecans. She could almost taste Gracie's pecan pies. When she first arrived in Cartersville, Georgia, the leaves on the trees, especially the maples, were a brilliant array of colors—red, orange and yellow. She was in love. She thought he loved her, too. Life was beautiful. But the beauty was short-lived.

Why did everything always take her thoughts back to Schooner? Winter was well on the way, but in a few months, new life would spring forth with tender new leaves on the trees. As if magic, the world would once again look alive with gorgeous purple wisteria and yellow Carolina Jasmine. The dark, dead winter would be forgotten. *So goes life.* In time, Schooner

Alexander would be wiped from her memory, as if he never existed. Bitter tears rolled down her cheeks. She reached in her coat pocket for a handkerchief. There wasn't a handkerchief, but she felt something else. Pulling it out, she looked in her hand and saw she was holding her wedding ring. Sweet Carly had slipped it in there. Sliding it on her finger, she held out her hand and admired the tiny stones. She knew, even when Carly tried to convince her otherwise, that it was no more valuable than a prize out of a Cracker Jack box. But it was precious to her the night Schooner placed it on her finger.

If only she could forget! Yet, the scenario in the backroom of the Bottoms Up Bar . . . the rooming house . . . the night of their wedding. . . and the shocking revelation from Miss Jane—" Her thoughts never got that far without tears freely falling. What a dunce she was to think a fellow as handsome as Schooner Alexander could fall for a little nobody like her. She had to get him out of her mind. Had she forgotten what a louse he was? How many girls had he fooled into going into a smoke-filled barroom, believing there was a wedding chapel in the back room? Probably only one. Who else would be so gullible?

Recognizable sights came into view. She'd soon be home. Her thoughts turned to Grandpa. *Sweet Grandpa*! She swiped her tears with the sleeve of her blouse. It was wrong of her not to let him know she was alive and well. Perhaps, not well, for she'd never be well again—but he deserved to know she was alive. Hadn't her mother caused him a lifetime of heartache without her adding to his troubles? But wouldn't it hurt him worse to know the truth about her?

How she wished she could walk up to the door of Nine Gables and see Garth and Gracie holding out open arms, welcoming her home. But that wouldn't happen. She'd been a great disappointment and there was no way she'd ever be able to make it up to them. The thought of going back and seeing the hurt on their faces was almost more than she could bear. By now, their wounds should be healing, leaving tender scars. It wouldn't be fair to re-open the wounds.

But Grandpa was different. He had to know the truth, even if the knowledge cut to the bone.

It was dark by the time the bus let her off in front of Nine Gables. The lights were on and it looked even more magnificent than when she left. Through the window, she could see Garth reading the newspaper. The tears she'd struggled to hold inside, now gushed forth like a flowing well. "If only—" But it was useless to consider what might've been. The reality existed. She made a horrendous mistake and disappointed all those who meant the most to her.

She turned to walk to the shanty, when she heard a voice call out in the darkness. Her heart hammered. "Grandpa?"

"Ludie?"

Her eyes clouded and the outline disappeared. Had she imagined she heard his voice?

Heading toward the shanty, she stopped short. This time, she was certain she heard it.

"Lord, have mercy, if it ain't my baby. Thank you sweet Jesus, my baby's done come home."

She turned on her heels and ran toward the shadowy figure, sobbing uncontrollably. "Oh, Grandpa. I'm sorry. I'm so sorry."

A comforting arm wrapped around her, while his other arm held to the walking stick. "Shush up, pretty baby. All that matters is that you're home. My prayers have been answered. Come on now, and let Miz Gracie and Mr. Garth know the good news."

"No, Grandpa. I ain't good news. I can't face them."

"Why, sugar, that ain't no way to talk. They've missed you. We all have."

"No. Please. I can't. I came to see you and hope you'll allow me to live in the shanty, until I can find me a job and get on my feet—"

"What you talking about? That ain't gonna happen. Winter's coming, and—"

"Don't say that. Please don't say that."

"Sugar, are you all right? You're acting a bit peculiar. Wanting to stay in the shanty and not wanting to talk about winter leads me to thinking you got some mighty big troubles."I

Ludie followed her grandpa into the tiny cabin. Though it was dark, he strode over to the far side of the room, as if he could clearly see. Then lighting a lamp, he turned with open arms.

"Come here, child, and let your ol' Grandpa hold you in his arms. Law, I was about to decide the good Lord couldn't hear my cries. But I was wrong. He heard me, for sure. You look thin, sugar. Ain't you been eating good? You ain't sickly, are you?"

"I'm just fine, Grandpa."

"Chile', nothing sounds sweeter to ol' George's ears than to hear you call me Grandpa—and as true as it is—I reckon for both our sakes it would serve us better if'n you'd go back to calling me Uncle George, like all the white folks do."

"But it ain't fair."

"Shucks, chile, ain't nobody ever told you that life ain't always fair? Now, tell me where you been."

Convinced she owed him an explanation after running off, leaving him to worry, Ludie told all that she felt he could live with. Telling everything was not an option. Surely, the news would kill him.

George listened intently, allowing her to say everything she intended to say "Sugar, I had no right to ask. It don't matter where you been—all that matters is that you back where you b'long, with all the folks who love you."

"I thought Schooner loved me. I shoulda never left. He lied to me, Grand . . . I mean, Uncle George." She glanced about. "Grandpa, it sure feels good to be home."

"Home, my hind foot! You ain't home yet, sugar, and what have I told you about calling me Grandpa? It ain't right, and I won't have it. I'm jest Uncle George to you like I am to ever'body else. I had just gone outside to bring in wood for the fireplace when I heard the bus stop in front of Nine Gables. I thought at first I was dreaming. Come on, and I'll walk you home."

"I can't! Please, I wanna stay here. I'm too 'shamed to face Garth and Gracie."

"You ain't thinking straight, young'un. You gotta eat. Where you gonna get food?"

"I'll manage. I've done it before. Besides, Gran . . . Uncle George, you always throw the scraps to your hogs. You think maybe you could manage to slip me a morsel or two of the leftovers? I don't eat much."

"Well, it's plain to see you ain't been eating much, but baby, I can't let you do that."

"Why?" Ludie choked up with tears. "I shouldn't have come back. I thought you'd take care of me."

Ol' George sat in the straight-back cane chair and patted her on the back. "'At's exactly what Uncle George plans on doing. Taking care of his baby. Now stop whimperin' and wash your face, like I told you. Me and you is going to the big house and I ain't got time to dawdle. I got a job to do."

What did she have to lose? Surely, there was nothing she could do to cause Garth and Gracie to think any less of her, after the stunt she'd pulled. "Stupid, stupid, stupid," she whispered under her breath as she poured water from the pitcher into the ceramic bowl. Glaring into the small mirror above the washstand, she splashed the cold water on her face. Then, speaking to the image in the mirror, she screeched, "You've ruined everything. I wish you were dead."

Uncle George was already outside. She shuddered at the harshness in his voice when he called her by her whole name.

"Eliza Clementine Graham! I said it's time to go. Me and you ain't ones to shirk our duties and right now I got a duty to gather firewood and it's yo' duty to face up to the folks who took you in to love you like their own flesh and blood. I won't stand for you dissin' nobody, 'specially not Mr. Garth and Miz Gracie."

Uncle George had never raised his voice at her . . . well, not since she was a child, anyway, and she reckoned he had plenty of reason to yell at her back then. Drying her face, she whimpered, "Coming!"

George stopped at the woodpile and with a wave of his hand, directed her toward the kitchen door. "Well . . . go on in."

"I'll just wait over there by the door steps 'til you get in the wood, so we can go in together."

"Nothing doing. We didn't leave together. Now git."

"Please, Uncle George. I can't face them. I don't know what to say."

"You can start off by tellin' the truth, and I reckon you the onliest one who knows what that is."

Ludie placed her hand over her chest. "If my heart beats any faster, it's gonna beat outta my chest." Seeing Grandpa wasn't changing his mind, she lowered her head and ambled toward the house.

Once inside, she burst into tears, recalling the last conversation she had, standing in that very spot. Grandpa was wrong. She had no right to be there. As she turned to leave, she heard an ear-splitting, sharp scream.

Gracie came running toward her with tears flowing down her cheeks and arms opened wide. "Oh, m'goodness, you're home. We've missed you, sweet girl. We've all missed you."

Hearing the commotion, Garth came running down the stairs and into the kitchen. He wrapped his arms around both Gracie and Ludie. "Thank the Lord, our prayers have been answered."

Ludie pushed away. "No. You don't understand I don't deserve to be here. I should never have come back. You tried to warn me, and I was too stubborn to listen. What I done was sinful and I'll pay for it rest of my life. I shouldn't have come back."

Garth's brow furrowed. "You're wrong, sweetheart. You're here because God led you here. We love you but He loves you more."

"No! You only believe that because you don't know what I've done. God knows everything. I'm no good and He knows it. I ain't got no right to sit at your table, but I ain't too proud to admit I'm hungry. So if it ain't asking too much, I could eat a morsel or two. I'll sit on the back steps and eat it and then I'll leave. Grandpa was wrong—" She slapped her hand over her mouth.

Garth said, "Honey, who are you calling Grandpa?"

"Did I say Grandpa?"

Gracie said, "That's what it sounded like to me, too."

Ludie shrugged. "That's funny. And now I clean forgot what I was fixin' to say. I reckon I'll be leaving now."

Garth said, "Leaving? But you just got here. You can't turn around and walk out of our lives again without an explanation."

"After all the hateful things I said before I left, you still want me to stay?

Gracie frowned. "Honey, it's true that we were upset when you told us you were going away with . . . with that boy. But you made your decision, and perhaps we were wrong to judge him. I'm sure he is as wonderful as you said he was. When can we meet him?"

Garth said, "I don't see a ring. Does that mean you didn't marry him?"

"I had a ring. I sold it."

"Sold it? I don't understand."

Gracie's gaze locked with her husband's. "Garth, dear, this is no time to demand explanations. Ludie is home. Isn't that enough?"

He nodded, and hugged his adopted daughter once more. "Of course it is. Sorry, hon."

Gracie said, "Your room is just as you left it."

"How many children are living here, now?"

"Only Mercy and Olene."

Garth's lip lifted in a grin. "But I dare you to call her Olene. She insists her name is Swifty. It's what her father called her before he was killed. She's a handful. In fact, she reminds us of you, with her strong convictions."

"I believe that's just another way of saying she's a stubborn kid. Right? How old is she?"

"Six, but she thinks she's sixteen."

"What about Josie, Ben, Jennie and Daniel?"

"Josie and Ben's mother remarried and was able to take them back home, Jennie and Daniel's grandparents live near Troy, so they were sent to live at the Baptist Children's Home there, making it easier for the elderly grandparents to visit. Mercy has been quite lonesome. She'll be so excited to discover you're home."

Home! What a beautiful word.

Hearing the voices in the kitchen, Mercy came running downstairs, and jumped into Ludie's arms. "I knew you'd come back. Didn't I tell you, Mama? Didn't I tell you she'd come home?"

CHAPTER 24

From the moment Ludie arrived home, Gracie had plenty of questions but Garth suggested they be patient and allow her to tell only what she felt comfortable sharing. After all, it was obvious that the old boy had broken her heart and left her. She would require time to heal without being bombarded with questions.

Ludie had never been one to brood before, and although she did a good job attempting to put on a happy face, Gracie saw straight through the facade. She needed to meet a nice fellow who could help her put the past behind her, and Gracie knew just the one who could do it. If only she had asked for his phone number.

A week after Ludie arrived home, Uncle George came into the mansion with the day's mail. Gracie went through the small stack of envelopes, then stopped and stared when a church's return address caught her attention. It was addressed to Ludie.

When Garth came home for lunch, she sneaked it out of her pocket. "What do you think, Garth? Should we give it to her?"

"Of course, you should give it to her. For crying out loud, Gracie, it's her mail and it's from a church. To tell the truth, I can hardly wait for you to give it to her."

"But what if she doesn't tell us what's in it?"

He winked. "Then, we won't know, will we?"

"Oh, Garth. I know you think I'm nosey. But all I want is to know that she's okay and if there's something in this letter that reveals that, I hope she'll choose to share it."

Gracie waited until after lunch to pull out the envelope, for fear there could be information inside that might cause her to lose her appetite. When Ludie stood to clear the table, Gracie pulled it out and laid it on the table. "This came for you, today, dear."

Garth and Gracie exchanged glances. Then seeing a smile come across Ludie's face, Gracie felt the muscles in her shoulders relax.

Ludie said, "He wants to come here."

The tension in Gracie's muscles returned. "Uh . . . I suppose you're talking about the young man the kids called, 'Sooner?'"

Ludie bit her lip. "Schooner. His name is Schooner, and no. I hope I never see him again."

Garth let out a grateful sounding sigh. "Then you shouldn't have to, sweetheart."

Gracie knew Garth might not approve, but she could stand it no longer. "But why would his letter be in a church envelope?"

"Oh, this isn't from Schooner. It's from Johnny."

"Johnny who?"

"A preacher I dated a few times."

Gracie's brow shot up. "A preacher? But we thought it—"

Garth stopped her. "It doesn't matter what we thought. We've been wrong before—haven't we, dear?"

Gracie nodded. "Of course."

Ludie said, "He says he's been accepted at the New Orleans Seminary, and will move there in the Spring. He's asked if I'd mind him coming here for a visit."

Gracie's heart sank. Not that she had anything against preachers, for she didn't. But Alexander was so perfect for Ludie, and from what he'd told them, Ludie had thought so too, at one time. After Garth admonished her for wanting to interfere, she reluctantly agreed to stay out of Ludie's private affairs.

That evening, Ludie was in her room and Gracie called Garth aside to pour out her fears. "The preacher entering the picture changes the dynamics."

"What dynamics?"

"Don't you think he'd want her to know that he's crazy about her? She could make a terrible mistake that could affect her life if the preacher enters the picture now."

"No, Gracie. You promised."

"But that was before we knew there was another fellow trying to woo her. What if she falls in love with the preacher?"

"Then we'll be happy for her. Won't we, Gracie?"

Letters came every day for Ludie, with the name Johnny

McLanders in the top left-hand corner. It was the same handwriting, but no longer were they concealed in a church envelope.

The change in Ludie's temperament seemed bittersweet to Gracie. Not that she wasn't glad to see a positive change from moody to pleasant. Yet, pleasant was a far cry from being happy, and Gracie was sure she knew the one who could make her happy. Why did she make the promise not to tell Ludie about Alex? Now that they'd learned she had been dating the preacher during her absence, Garth was finally convinced she didn't marry that Sooner fellow.

Ludie read silently, then folded the letter. "He's coming."

"Coming? The Preacher?"

"Yes. I know you and Garth will like him. Miz Carly was crazy about him."

"Carly? Who is Miz Carly, dear?"

Her face blushed as if the word slipped out of her mouth.

"A friend. A really good friend who introduced me to Johnny."

Garth glared at his wife and shook his head slightly. She had no trouble understanding his silent instructions. He said, "Ludie, I'm sure he's a fine young man, and we'd be delighted for him to stay with us while he's in town."

"Thank you, I'll tell him."

Gracie flinched. Why was Garth making it so easy for her to become entangled with the wrong man?

When they were alone, Gracie gave her husband a tongue-lashing. "What were you thinking, inviting him to stay here?"

"What better way of getting to know him, Gracie. If he's planning on courting my daughter, I want to know what kind of fellow he is."

The letters continued to come in the following days and Gracie wasn't sure how long she could hold out before telling Ludie what she promised not to tell.

Several days later, Mercy and Olene came running in the house, shouting, "He's here! The preacher is here."

Gracie reprimanded them both for not acting lady-like. "Go upstairs and let Ludie know, while I greet him at the door."

He was thirty minutes early, and the chicken had just begun to fry. Of all times for Garth to be late. Olene came running back down the stairs and fell. Could things get any worse? Not knowing whether to answer the door, watch the chicken or pick up a wailing child, she decided to yell for help. "LUDIE!"

Ludie, unaccustomed to hearing Gracie raise her voice, came running down the stairs in a panic and tripped over Olene at the bottom of the stairs, and fell, breaking a heel from her shoe. She hurried back upstairs to change shoes.

Gracie had met Johnny at the door, and invited him into the parlor. It was then that Garth came home and shouted, "Where's the smoke coming from?" Without waiting for an answer, he ran into the kitchen, grabbed the skillet and poured a box of salt over the grease fire.

Mercy had come back downstairs and was standing in the doorway to the parlor, staring at the frightened-looking young man. "Are you my sister's boyfriend?"

When he swallowed hard, his Adam's apple looked too large for his thin neck. "Uh . . . yes. Yes, I suppose I am." He jumped up when Ludie entered the room.

"It's good to see you, Johnny."

"Likewise."

"How have you been?"

"Fair to middling, I guess. And you?"

"Good."

Standing there wringing her hands, Ludie tried to think of something more to say, when Garth and Gracie entered. After the introductions, Garth said, "Reverend McLanders, I'm afraid you won't have the pleasure of enjoying my wife's cooking tonight, since we've had a minor accident in the kitchen. But we'll all go over to the Samson Cafe for supper. It'll be a nice outing. They serve a very good T-Bone. Do you like steak?"

Johnny nodded and mumbled something that Ludie hoped was in the affirmative. She breathed easier, now that she didn't feel she would be totally responsible for carrying on the conversation alone. Garth was sure to have plenty of questions and it would be interesting to see if Johnny could answer them all in one-word sentences.

The waitress brought out the steaks and they were just as good as Garth promised. She sat back smiling, as she followed the conversation. Garth was doing just fine.

He said, "Gracie tells me you're planning on going to the Seminary."

"Yessir."

"When will you leave."

"January."

"That's not long off. I believe Ludie said you turned down the offer of a church. Where is your home?"

"Georgia."

"I see. So I gather you'll be staying home until school starts."

"No sir."

"No?" Garth shot a glance toward Ludie, which she understood as a plea for help. Suddenly, what was an agonizing situation when she was trying to squeeze a conversation out of him, now seemed quite humorous as she watched Garth attempting to pull out an entire sentence.

Wanting to help Garth, she said, "Johnny, if you aren't going home, I suppose you'll be going on to New Orleans to get settled in an apartment before school starts."

"Maybe."

"Garth said, "Maybe you'd like to elaborate?"

Gracie covered her mouth with her napkin to hide her smile.

"I would, sir. From the moment I met your daughter, I knew she was the kind of woman I'd be pleased to marry."

Ludie grinned. She knew what the others thought he was

going to say, but they were wrong. It was simply his way of paying her a compliment.

He continued. "Any man would feel the same way."

There! She knew it. Smiling, she said, "Thank you, Johnny. That's very sweet. Don't you think so, Garth?"

His lip curled. "He said a mouthful, all right."

"But that's not all, sir. Mr. Graham, would you have objections to me marrying your daughter?"

Garth chuckled as if it were a joke. "I don't know you, son. She does. Why don't you ask her if that's what she wants. If it is, I won't stand in the way."

Gracie covered her mouth. "No!" She lowered her head. "I mean, no, this is awfully quick. Suppose you two think about it before making such a big decision. Ludie is still in school. You're a good bit older. There's no need to rush into such a big decision."

"Begging your pardon, ma'am, but it's all I've thought about since the day I met her."

He slid back from the table and dropped to his knees beside Ludie's chair. "Elizabeth Clementine Graham, will you give me the honor of being my wife?"

She glanced around and realized everyone in the cafe was watching—waiting for her answer. A blush warmed her face. "Uh . . . "Yes?"

Everyone in the building stood and clapped.

Johnny picked up her left hand and slid a ring on her third finger.

Garth looked at his wife and handed her a handkerchief to catch the tears.

Mercy and Olene were obviously delighted that there'd soon be a wedding. Mercy said, "Can we be flower girls, please, please, pretty please?"

Ludie gave a slight shrug. "I don't know . . . I mean . . . yes. Yes, you can. I don't know what I'm saying."

Gracie picked up on the opportunity. "Of course, you don't, dear. It all happened so quickly. You'll have plenty of time to think about things later. There's no rush."

Johnny said, "Actually, there is, Mrs. Graham. I'd like to be married before I start to school, and we'll need to go to New Orleans and find a place to live."

"But you can't!"

The shock on Gracie's face didn't escape Garth. "This has come as a surprise. We had no idea things had progressed to this point between you two. But if this is what you both want, then Gracie and I are happy for you."

Ludie said, "I don't like having so many people staring. Could we please go, now?"

CHAPTER 25

After arriving back at Nine Gables, Mercy and Olene went upstairs to get their baths. Gracie wanted to sit in the parlor with Johnny and Ludie, but Garth insisted she allow them time alone, to make plans.

Trudging up the stairs to their bedroom, she grumbled. "That's exactly why I didn't want to leave them alone. They have no business making wedding plans."

"Honey, I realize he isn't your pick, but you aren't the one who gets to choose."

"Don't you understand, Garth? She didn't choose. She settled. She's been hurt deeply by the only two fellows she's ever cared about. First by Alex and then by Sooner. She said she'd never get married, and now, all of a sudden she takes the first man to ask her? I suppose she thinks she'll be safe with a preacher, but I have news for her. Marrying someone she doesn't love will be the worst hurt of all."

"But you don't know that she doesn't love him?"

"Yes, I do and if you'd pay attention, you'd know it, too. It's obvious."

The only ones talking at the breakfast were Olene and Mercy and Gracie had to correct them for acting silly at the table. After they quieted down, the only sounds were the eating utensils hitting the China plates.

When everyone was finished, Johnny said, "Thank you for your hospitality. I'll go get my bag and be leaving."

Gracie perked up at the thought that Ludie might have come to her senses. "Leaving so soon?"

"Yes ma'am. I thought Clemmie might like to go help choose the apartment, but she insisted that whatever I found would be fine."

"We all call her Ludie. She's always been called Ludie."

"Yes ma'am. But I call her Clemmie."

Gracie felt her shoulders stiffen.

He wrapped his arm around Ludie and said, "I'll be counting off the next seventeen days."

Ludie nodded. "Have a nice trip."

Gracie's brow meshed together. "Wait. What's happening in seventeen days?"

The shy fellow who barely said two words when he arrived, now seemed more than willing to talk. "Our wedding date."

"But that isn't enough time to plan a wedding."

Ludie spoke up, saying she didn't want a big wedding. They'd get married at Nine Gables, with family only. "His father is a preacher, so he'll perform the ceremony."

Garth said, "I agree with Gracie. And seventeen days isn't even enough time to plan a honeymoon."

With a shrug, Ludie said, "I don't want a honeymoon. We'll have a quiet wedding, and then set up housekeeping in the apartment Johnny gets for us."

They stood on the porch and watched as Johnny drove down the long, dirt road on his way to New Orleans.

Gracie's heart was so crushed, she knew if she said another word, she'd start bawling. She was heartbroken the day Ludie told them she was running away with Sooner, a boy she hardly knew. But this felt no better. It was as if Ludie had given up on love. Had Alex hurt her that bad?

She followed her up to her room. "Honey, you don't seem very happy for a girl who is planning to marry the man she's in love with. Is there a reason?"

"Gracie, I know you married for love, but you've said you didn't love Garth when you first met him. Yet, you learned to love him. Plenty of mail-order brides have learned to love their husbands in time. I'm sure I shall, too."

"Oh, honey, how can I make you understand?" As soon as she asked the question, the answer came to her. Sometimes promises have to be broken and the promise she made could ruin Ludie's life if she refused to tell. "Honey, there's something I need to tell you, that I wish I'd told you weeks ago. The only reason I didn't was because I made him a promise. But I know now that he'd release me from that promise if he knew what was about to take place."

"What are you trying to say?"

"Alex came here looking for you. Sweetheart, I know he hurt you badly. He told us all about it, but he's very remorseful. He told us he loves you very much and regrets it took him so long to realize how much you mean to him."

Ludie rolled her eyes. "I know you don't approve of Johnny and I don't know why. He's a real gentleman and will treat me well. I plan to go through with this, Gracie, so making up a story about a fictional lover won't work."

"Fictional? Did you not hear me? I said Alex. You loved him once, but he was mixed up. He loves you, darling, and Garth and I both were very impressed with him."

"I can understand why. He's a marvelous story-teller. I'm sure you were entertained, but I've never known an Alex."

"Sure you have. He wouldn't have lied. He's crazy about you."

"Fine. Somewhere there's a boy named Alex who is crazy. That part I can believe." She quickly changed the subject and began talking about New Orleans and Gracie began to understand the thrill of seeing New Orleans appealed to her, more than the idea of getting married.

The tension between Ludie and Gracie became more intense as the wedding day drew closer.

Gracie met Garth for lunch the next day at the Samson Cafe. She could hardly eat for crying. "Garth, I don't know why you aren't as upset over this as I am. She's sixteen, for crying out loud. As her parents, don't we have a right to stop her from ruining her life?"

"And lose her forever? We tried to stop her from running off with that other fellow and look where that got us. No, Gracie, we have to let her go and pray that in time, she'll grow to love him. She certainly could do worse—in fact, she did. Remember? I agree, Alexander was very personable and won our hearts, but this is not about us. Johnny has a future and he'll be good to her, of that I'm sure."

"I know Alex was telling the truth. But I can't understand why Ludie is pretending she never knew him. She's stubborn, for sure, and doesn't always think things through before reacting, but we've always been able to count on her to tell us the truth. I can't imagine why she'd lie about knowing him."

"Think about it, Gracie. Alexander admitted that he hurt her. I have a feeling he hurt her more than you or I will ever know. I'm not convinced that she is lying."

"What are you saying? You think Alex lied?"

"I don't think either of them is lying. It appears to me that Ludie purposely chose to wipe him from her memory, and maybe we should do the same thing."

"You really think she loved so deeply that she's unconsciously put up a shield to keep from ever falling in love that way again?"

"I don't know. All I know is that she's made up her mind and I'll guarantee you that if we tried to interfere at this point, we'd live to regret it. Let's try to be happy for her—or at least pretend we are, for her sake."

"I want to, Garth, but how can I be happy when I don't believe she is? The wedding is only a week away, and she hasn't even mentioned wanting to buy a dress to get married in. That isn't normal."

He hee-hawed. "When has anyone ever called our daughter normal? Why don't you go shopping this afternoon and pick out something pretty for her to wear. If nothing else, it will show her that you are supporting her in her decision."

"But I'm not supporting her."

"Gracie, get over it."

His blunt words caused her to want to react, and she would have—except she knew he was right.

She'd go over to Mr. Merchant's Dry Goods and pick out the prettiest dress he had in stock.

After arriving home, she laid out a lovely lavender suit with little seed pearls sewn onto the collar. Then pulling out a pair of white gloves and white pumps, she laid them on the bed with the dress, and called Ludie to come upstairs.

Ludie said, "I suppose that's what you want me to wear when Johnny and I get married?"

"Don't you like it?"

"It's nice. Thank you, but you shouldn't have bothered. I plan to wear my navy skirt and white blouse."

Gracie felt the ire rising. "Of all the ungrateful little—" She sucked in a deep breath and slowly let it out. "That's fine, dear. I can take it back."

"Don't bother. If that's what you want me to wear, I'll wear it."

"If it's what I want? Ludie Graham if you were really concerned about what I want you wouldn't be rushing into this sham of a marriage. You don't love him and I'm not sure he loves you. I think he feels he needs a wife and you made yourself available."

"Are you through?"

Gracie burst into tears. "I'm sorry. Honey, I'm so sorry. I don't know what made me say that. You should wear what you're most comfortable wearing, and the navy skirt looks beautiful on you." She smiled, "It's expected of the bride to feel a little panicky days before making a lifetime vow, but you're the calm one, and I'm the one with the wedding jitters. Please forget what I said. Of course, he loves you."

She was surprised when Ludie smiled. "No, he doesn't. He thinks he does, but he doesn't know what it feels like to be in love. I have something to compare it with, but I'm not looking for love. I can live without it."

"Oh, my precious Ludie, did Sooner hurt you that much?"

"Schooner! His name is Schooner. And to answer your question—yes, he hurt me more than you'll ever know, but maybe he did me a favor."

"I don't understand."

"No one will ever get the chance to hurt me again, because I won't allow myself to be so vulnerable. I was a fool."

Gracie's eyes widened. "Are you saying you're calling off the wedding?"

Ludie's face pinched into a frown. "Calling it off? Of course not. Johnny must know that I don't love him. I've never said that I did, yet he's gonna take me to New Orleans. I've always wanted to go there."

They looked up and saw Garth standing there.

Gracie said, "I didn't hear you come in, dear."

"Seems I came in just in time. Is that what this is all about, Ludie? You're getting married to have someone take you to New Orleans? For crying out loud, girl, if you want to go that bad, I'll take you myself and we'll find you a room in a boarding house. But don't destroy a young man's life for a trip to a place you have no business being in the first place."

Gracie's jaw dropped. "You'll do no such thing. It's one thing to have her there with a husband to watch out for her, but I'll not have her left alone in that wicked place."

Ludie appeared amused. "There's two sides to everything I don't think New Orleans is the exception. From what I've read, it's a training ground where both saints and sinners are schooled. I reckon I can decide after I get there in which school I prefer to obtain my education."

Gracie burst into tears. "Shame on you, Elizabeth Clementine. The Good Lord doesn't take to such jesting."

"I'm sorry, but Gracie, I have to get away from here, and although I know Garth would take me to New Orleans, I agree with you—I don't need to be in the city, alone. I don't even want to. I'd feel much safer knowing Johnny would be coming home every day after school. Besides, I'd have someone to show me around, take me out to eat whenever we could afford it. I'd have someone to change a tire, help pay the rent, etcetera. I'd grocery shop, cook and keep house for him. I could even get a job waiting tables to help with finances. We'll be fine."

Unable to breathe, Gracie rolled her eyes and hurried from the room. She'd said all she knew to say.

Garth followed her out the door and wrapped his arms around her. "Honey, have you thought that this may be how our Heavenly Father feels when he directs us in the right path but we rebel and choose to go another way? He has a will for our lives, and it's perfect, but he doesn't force his will on us."

"What's your point? Are you saying we should sit idly by and allow her to ruin her life?"

"No, you missed the point. I'm saying we aren't God. His way is always right. Are you sure we're right? What if Johnny is the one God has chosen for our Ludie?"

"Don't be ridiculous."

Ludie stepped out of her room, into the hall. "Would you two stop arguing? I can hear every word, and all that bickering isn't changing a thing. I'm getting married, and that's that." She ran down the stairs and headed down the long hallway.

Gracie yelled, "Where are you going?"

"For a walk in the woods to clear my head." The door slammed.

Gracie was cooking supper and squalling. How did things get in such a mess? When the phone rang, she cleared her voice, then answered.

Minutes later, she hung up and ran in the parlor. "Quick, Garth, help me straighten up in here. Everything is a mess. I don't know how many times I've warned Olene and Mercy about leaving puzzles strewn out on the floor. Call them to come pick up the pieces."

He laid down his paper. "What's got you in such a dither?"

"Alex. He's coming. I've invited him for supper."

"What? Even after you told him Ludie was getting married?" He brow creased. "You did tell him, didn't you"

"Of course not, silly. I'm sure he would've been too hurt to come if I had told him."

He rubbed the back of his neck. "Gracie, Gracie, Gracie. What have you done?"

"Stop gabbing and help me. He'll be here at six and I haven't even begun supper."

"Ludie has told you she doesn't know him. This could turn out to be a very embarrassing situation for them both. He's holding out hopes for a girl who doesn't even remember him. You should've stayed out of it."

Gracie had no time for second-guessing her decision. Surely, God orchestrated the whole thing. Why else would Alex call, now? Besides, what was done was done. She took pork chops from the Frigidaire, made tomato gravy, biscuits and opened up cans of beans and squash that she canned in the summer. She lifted the lid to the cake taker and was relieved to see enough pound cake left for supper. She kept watching the clock. The sun was going down, and Ludie was still not home. Then, hearing the front door open, she laid down the oven mitt and ran to meet her in the hall.

"Honey, please go upstairs, wash up and put on that pretty pink gingham dress hanging in your closet."

"I don't have a pink gingham."

"You do now. I saw it in a store window last week, and bought it, hoping you'd have a special occasion to wear it."

"Thank you, Gracie. I can hardly wait to see it, but I'll try it on after we eat."

"I'd like for you to wear it to supper, dear. Do you mind?"

"No, but who's coming?"

"A friend of your father's. Now, hurry. It's almost six, now."

After Ludie left for her room, Gracie mulled over her words. She hadn't told a lie. Had she? Garth was impressed with Alex, so it wasn't a stretch to say they were friends. Ludie claimed she knew no one named Alex. In a matter of minutes, Gracie would know whether it was Ludie or Alex with selective memory. Was he remembering what he wanted to remember—or was Ludie forgetting what she wanted to forget. She knew Garth wouldn't approve of what she was doing, but she had to know. It was her last attempt at trying to prevent Ludie from making a huge mistake.

Ludie dressed and walked into the dining room when she heard the doorbell rang. When Garth started toward the door, Gracie yelled, "Garth, dear, I need you in the kitchen. Let Ludie answer the door."

CHAPTER 26

Ludie's breath caught in her throat. "You! What are you doing here?"

His jaw dropped. "Ludie? I was about to ask you same thing."

"I live here." She slammed the door in his face. Holding back the tears, she walked back into the dining room.

Gracie and Garth exchanged glances. Curious, Gracie walked to the kitchen door and peered down the hall. "Honey, who was at the door? I didn't hear anyone come in."

"Just some creep at the wrong address."

Garth shrugged. "Creep? That doesn't sound like you, hon. We thought it might be—"

Before he could finish, Gracie stopped him. "Garth thought that might be his friend that we're expecting for supper."

"No. He's no friend."

The animosity in her voice was enough to make Gracie run down the hall. She had to catch him. She couldn't let him walk away. Not now. Even if Ludie didn't remember him, it was no sign a spark couldn't be lit at supper, once she got to know him. Any girl would be crazy not to go for such a handsome, sweet fellow.

When she slung open the door, Alex was still standing there as if he had no intention of walking away.

"Come on in. I don't think Ludie recognized you. It's so good to see you again."

"I didn't know she was home."

"I had no way of contacting you."

"I know. I didn't have an address or phone number to give you. I can see she still hates me, but I can't give up on her."

"Fiddlesticks, she doesn't hate you." Gracie was beginning to feel there was much more going on than Ludie had indicated. Alex followed her into the dining room.

Ludie glared at Garth. "He's . . . he's your friend?"

Garth shook hands with Alex and nodded. "Yes, he is. Ludie, you do remember Alex, don't you?"

"Is that who he told you he is? He's a liar."

Gracie felt her face grow hot. "Elizabeth Clementine, I don't know what's got into you, but I think you owe Alexander an apology."

"First of all, let me inform you that if he told you his name is Alex, he lied to you." Then as if a thought suddenly caused her lip to split into a craggy smile, she muttered. *Alexander.* "You called him Alexander?"

"Yes. So you do remember."

Alex said, "Please, let me explain. "Ludie, I came looking for you. I understand if you don't want to talk to me, but please allow me to speak. When your father introduced himself as Graham, I answered with my last name. When your mother referred to me as Alex, I knew she assumed Alexander was my first name, but to keep from embarrassing her, I let it go. After all, I learned you weren't here, and that's what I came for."

"Schooner, I don't know what you hoped to accomplish by looking for me. Surely, you know how I feel after what you did to me. So, if you'll kindly leave after supper, we'll all be better off."

Garth reached over and clasped his hand in his wife's. Tears mulled in her eyes. She said, "You're . . . you're Schooner? Oh, my goodness. What have I done? I'm so sorry, Ludie. I didn't know."

"Forget it, Gracie. I understand how you could've been fooled. He's good at fooling people. I've suddenly lost my appetite. Schooner, please join me on the porch. I have a lot of questions that I'd like answered before you head back to Cartersville."

He glanced over at Gracie, as he shoved back his chair. "Excuse me, please. The food looks delicious, but I have no right to sit at your table." He followed Ludie to the porch.

"Ludie, please let me explain."

"There's nothing to explain. Your actions were quite explanatory." As much as she didn't want to give him the opportunity to lie again, something inside her desperately wanted to hear what he had to say. Her teeth ground together. Then with a shrug, she said, "Have at it. If you can top the last lies you told me, this should be quite a story."

When his voice quaked, she grinned. He was doing a great job of faking remorse.

Ludie had trouble discerning whether it was her eagerness to believe him, or if what she was hearing could possibly be true, but she listened intently with no thoughts of interrupting.

He told her about the way he grew up assuming no one ever told the truth, but twisted it to fit their need. His father never held a job, and taught his boys to lie to the law when they'd ask questions concerning the moonshine still. He'd dated lots of girls, but the girls he dated could out-lie him. "Then you came along. You were like no one I'd ever known." His brothers thought up the wedding scenario and encouraged him to go along. "After I went through with it, I realized what I felt for you was real, and that you loved me, too. I was angry with myself for listening to my brothers, but I knew if I told you the marriage was a sham that you'd hate me."

She sat unmoving while he talked so fast, he could barely draw a breath. "I hurt so bad, I couldn't stand it. I realized too late how much I wanted that marriage to be real. I wanted to be your husband, but it was too late. Miss Jane filled your head with the truth about me and my family and I knew after that I'd lost you for good."

"You were right, Schooner. So why did you come looking for me?"

"For two reasons. The first is because I discovered that I love you too much to give up so easily. The second is because of my sixth-grade schoolteacher."

When he began to open up, Ludie sat quietly and allowed him to spill his guts—not that she believed a single word that he was saying.

"Sweetheart, I don't blame you for hating me, and everything Miz Jane told you about us Alexanders is true."

Her jaw jutted forward. "Don't call me sweetheart. I'm not your sweetheart."

"I'm sorry . . . sorry for offending you and dreadfully sorry that you don't want to be my sweetheart, but I understand. You have a great family and I'm a nobody. Always have been. I didn't start out life choosing to be a low-life, but after the robbery, I gave up on trying to be somebody. Everybody in town knew what happened and I reckon after that we were feared almost as much as the James brothers, or at least Brute wanted to think so."

"Robbery? What are you talking about?"

He ran his fingers through his dark curls, and Ludie had to remind herself that he was a louse and a liar.

"You mean . . . Miz Jane didn't tell you?"

Ludie wanted to pretend she wasn't interested in hearing, but her curiosity wouldn't permit her to stop him. The more he talked, the more she realized how blessed she was that the marriage was a fake. At least she wouldn't have to file for a divorce. "And how old were you when this alleged robbery took place?"

"Nothing alleged about it. It was in all the papers. At the time,

Brute was seventeen; Ox was fifteen; I was eleven and Grander was nine. We'd been helping out at the Still, and were loading into the truck to go home. Brute had a dilapidated old truck, which he and Ox used to transport the moonshine. I reckon it was around nine-thirty at night and Brute was waiting for me and Grander to crawl in the back. I made the comment that I wished I had a bicycle so I could get me a paper route and make some money. Brute laughed out loud and I remember it made me mad that he was laughing at me, although I should've been used to it. Then he said, that I'd given him a good idea. I was hoping he was about to say he'd buy me a bicycle—but that wasn't what he was thinking."

Ludie's lip curled in a smirk. "So I suppose you thought robbing a store would be a much faster way to make money than delivering newspapers."

The sadness on his face made her wish she hadn't been so sarcastic, though she had plenty of reason to be.

For a moment it looked as if he wanted to end the conversation. He breathed in, and said, "No, it had nothing to do with a paper route."

"Then what?"

"Not what, but who. I'll never forget the way Brute clasped his hand on my shoulder and whispered, 'Swear you won't tell, Schooner, but I know an easy way for us all to get some cash. You could get that bicycle, but you can't tell nobody. Nobody! You hear what I'm saying?' I was always too afraid of Brute to refuse him anything. I nodded, and that's when he said the old fellow at Grimsley's Grocery always left around ten o'clock with a bank bag full of the days' receipts. I had a feeling he'd already talked it over with Ox and Grander. It wasn't so much that he wanted to let me in on the plan, as it was a threat of what they'd do to me if I didn't keep my mouth shut.

Ox was all excited and said, 'Let's do it tonight.' Brute agreed and said we'd drive around to the back where Grimsley always parked and he'd let Ox out of the car before the old man locked up.

The plan was for Ox to hide behind the outbuilding and Brute would stay behind the wheel of the truck in order to make a quick getaway. When Mr. Grimsley started to open his car door, Ox was to come from behind, hit him over the head with a soda bottle before the old man could see who hit him. Ox would then grab the bag, and Brute would speed away before Mr. Grimsley would come to."

Ludie rolled her eyes. "I ain't sure if you're bragging about how tough you and your brothers are or if you're trying to make me think less of you. But if that's the case, you can stop, because you've already hit rock-bottom in my little black book

.

CHAPTER 27

It seemed there was nothing left to say. Then in a low voice, Ludie smirked, "I had no idea that you and your family were so famous in Cartersville."

"Famous? Do you really think it gives me pleasure to tell you how rotten we Alexanders are? If you do, you're wrong. I detest talking about it. But I was told by a very wise person that I should tell you the truth, the whole truth, and nothing but the truth, and that's my intention. Just as Ox was about to hit Grimsley with the bottle, the old man swung around and grabbed it out of his hand and tripped him. Ox fell to the ground and Brute got scared an sped away. Naturally, when the police picked up Ox, they went straight for Brute. A trial was held and the whole town showed up. The verdict was guilty and the sentence was a year in the Reformatory School."

Ludie sat with her arms tightly crossed over her midsection. "Obviously the Reformatory School was a waste of time, since it didn't reform you."

When their gaze met, her thoughts frightened her. Why did he have to be so bad? Why couldn't he be the Schooner she thought he was? The Schooner she fell in love with?

He said, "I didn't go. Maybe you think what I'm about to tell you next is to try to make me look good, but I hold no such hopes. You've asked the outcome, and I'm gonna lay it out for you."

Schooner explained that when Brute told of his plan to rob Mr. Grimsley, he jumped out of the back of the truck and ran. He took a shortcut through a woman's yard, and she flipped on the porch light when she heard a noise. He said, "It scared me when she called my name and asked what I was doing out so late at night. Naturally, I couldn't tell her, but Mrs. Grimsley said she could tell I was in trouble. Said she was worried about me and if there was anything she could do to help me, to come by anytime and talk with her."

"Wait—you said Grimsley. Was she the old man's wife?"

He nodded. "Yep! But I didn't know that the boys were gonna get caught, so I thought she'd never know what I was running away from. And she didn't—until she got a call from her husband who was at the station booking my three brothers."

"Even nine-year-old Grander? He was sent off?"

"Even Grander. He's always been the adventurous one. He started stealing candy when he was a little bitty fellow and only got caught once. He got real good at it."

"Adventurous? That's not what I call it." Ludie could hardly believe what she was hearing.

"Well, no one ever called him a coward."

Was he so cruel that he thought knocking people over the head and stealing was something to be admired? Chills ran down her spine. And to think, she almost married into that gang of thieves. Swallowing hard, she realized it was only in her naive mind that she came close to marrying Schooner. Marrying her was never a part of his plan. So why was he back? Did he honestly figure if she was so gullible the first time, that he could fool her again?

"I can close my eyes at night and still hear them chanting, 'Coward, coward, Schooner is a coward,' when I jumped out and ran away from the truck. When they went to court, I wasn't charged since Mrs. Grimsley told the judge I was with her at the time the incident took place. I think Daddy was more ashamed of me than he was of them. He'd tell Mama, "He's from your side of the family.' It was true I looked like Mama and my brothers favored Daddy, but I knew that wasn't what he meant. I guess they were right about me, because the thought of poor Mr. Grimsley getting knocked over the head brought tears to my eyes. They were all stronger than me."

Ludie felt her heart softening, yet she couldn't allow him to hoodwink her again with his conniving lies. She stiffened her neck and said, "That's quite a story. You should write a book. But frankly, I don't care about your past, your present or your future, Schooner Alexander. However, I do have one question for you. You said there were two reasons why you came looking for me. I didn't believe the first reason, but I'm very curious about the second one. What does a schoolteacher have to do with you coming to find me?"

He tightened his lips and sat silent for what seemed like several minutes.

Assuming he had concluded she wouldn't be as easy to trick this time and was giving up, she smiled. "Just as I thought. Your second reason for coming was as bogus as your first."

"Not bogus, but you've made up your mind not to believe anything I say. Not that I blame you. Yet, I couldn't help hoping."

"Try me. I want to hear everything you came here to say."

Schooner stood and walked over to the edge of the porch and leaned against a post, his back to her. When he began to speak, his voice quivered and he stopped. She wondered if he was such a good actor that he could bring on the tears at will. Aggravated that she felt a lump forming in her throat, she reminded herself that she cried at movies, so the sympathy she was feeling had nothing to do with Schooner, but sad stories always made her cry. She was glad he wasn't facing her, since he might misinterpret her tears.

Her chin quivered as he told her that after she left, he was so distraught that he went to the only person who had ever believed in him—Mrs. Grimsley.

Schooner said while grieving over Ludie leaving, he remembered something Mrs. Grimsley said to him the night of the attempted robbery. "She hugged me when I started to leave her ght and told me she believed in me. Said I was m my brothers, but she made it sound like a good thing, at a time that I was still hearing the word 'coward' ringing in my ears. She told me if I ever needed to talk to someone, she'd always be ready to listen. I'll never forget her hugging me and telling me that she loved me. I'd never had anyone to tell me that. Not even Mama. So, when you left, I had never been so low. I needed help, and I thought of sweet old Mrs. Grimsley."

Ludie bit her lip as he shared how Mrs. Grimsley listened. He said she made him feel he wasn't a coward growing up, but he was a brave boy with strong convictions and stood up for what he believed to be right.

His face darkened. "I told her she was wrong. When Brute planned the fake wedding, I didn't want to go along with it, but the fellows began their chant, 'Coward, coward, Schooner is a coward.' Mrs. Grimsley told me the reason I didn't want to participate wasn't because I was a coward, but because I knew it was wrong. It was only when I finally agreed to go through with it that I became a coward, for not standing up for what I believed."

"Schooner, how do I know you're being truthful, now? You told me you were into manufacturing and distribution when I questioned you about your job. It was all a lie."

He caught his bottom lip between his teeth and shook his head. "Actually, that was true. I just didn't tell you I worked for Daddy, manufacturing moonshine and distributing it all over the county in five gallon jugs."

"So you're a moonshiner."

"No more. I turned in an application to work at the Cotton

Mill in Geneva and I was notified yesterday that I'm to start Monday morning."

Confused, Ludie's feeling wavered back and forth. Truth or lies? How could she know for sure? It was only after he said Mrs. Grimsley told him how much God loved him, and what he did next, that the doubts began to fade. Could he really share such a beautiful story about becoming a believer if it weren't true?

He said, "She prayed with me, and I've asked the Lord's forgiveness. I realized I'd been living my life in the flesh to please my brothers. I now choose to live by faith to please God. Do you understand what I'm trying to say?"

She pressed her lips into a tight line without acknowledging his question, but asked one of her own. "Is that all?"

"No. Then Mrs. Grimsley squeezed my hand and looking me in the eyes, she said, 'Now, Schooner, you have one more thing to do. You need to find the girl you wronged and ask her to forgive you. I promised her that I would." He leaned forward and met her eyes squarely. "Ludie Graham, I love you with all my heart, but what I did to you was so horrible, I can understand if you can't find it in your heart to forgive me."

She jumped up, grabbed his hand and pulled him into the parlor, where Garth and Gracie were sitting.

Gracie's jaw dropped when she saw Ludie smiling from ear to ear. She squealed, "Does this mean what I hope it means?"

Schooner, looking confused, lifted his shoulders in a shrug. "I don't know ma'am, but I hope if you're hoping the same thing I'm hoping, I hope we're right."

Ludie wrapped an arm around his waist. "It means Schooner has a job at the Cotton Mill and hopefully we can move into one of the Village houses after we're married. Gracie, I was wondering if you'd have time to go with me to shop for a wedding dress, Monday morning."

"Honey, we'll be standing at the door when the Bridal Shop opens."

Schooner grabbed Ludie and slung her in the air. "Hallelujah, little darlin'! My prayers have been answered."

Uncle George brought in a load of coal and emptied it into the copper scuttle. "What's this I hear?"

"We're getting married, Grandpa." She swallowed hard, her eyes searching the faces in the room. No one appeared to notice her blunder except Grandpa George, who seemed rather pleased.

Gracie sighed. "But Ludie, what about Johnny?"

"Don't worry about Johnny. I have a feeling God has somebody picked out for him. He didn't need to marry me and I needed to marry Schooner. The way I figure it, the Good Lord saw we were about to make an awful mistake so he took care of all our needs at the same time. Ain't God good, y'all?"

Grandpa George grinned. "More'n we'll ever know."

Made in the USA
Columbia, SC
09 February 2022

54951954R00157